CW01310753

SUBJEC

Jeffrey Thomas

01010011011101010110001001101010011001010110
00110111010000100000001100010011000100100000
01100010011110010010000001001010011001010110
01100110011001110010011001010111100100100000
01010100011010000110111101101101011000010111
0011

Welcome to the Subject 11 project.

We are currently seeking 10 individuals to participate in a research study. Participants shall receive a sum to be discussed during initial telephone interview. Interested parties should email us via our contact page, subject11.webs.com, providing their telephone number and a brief biography of approximately 100 words, describing themselves in terms of gender, age, race, and occupation if any. The study will take place in a series of abandoned buildings rented for this purpose. Note: subjects involved in this test may find themselves experiencing certain psychological distortions. They may experience lapses in memory regarding others and themselves. Subjects may even forget how long this test is supposed to go on for. And please disregard any additional people you may feel you've sighted in the complex, beyond those in the test group. We thank you for your interest in our research...

"Cutting right to the chase, *Subject 11* is one of the best novellas I've read all year. Jeffrey Thomas is at his best in this eerie story following a group of ten people (five women and five men) taking part in a mysterious experiment...The mysteries are enticing, and Thomas brings them together for an ending that is sure to linger long in the minds of readers."

- Justin Steele, THE ARKHAM DIGEST

"This book will mess with your mind, and you will feel that you have left a bit of your sanity behind after you finish... it is right at the top of my list for best story so far this year. You will not be disappointed and I give it my highest recommendation."

- LITERARY MAYHEM

Subject 11 © 2014 by Jeffrey Thomas.

All Rights Reserved.

Cover photo and cover design by the author.

Author's photo by Colin Thomas.

Subject 11 was originally published as a limited edition hardcover book by Delirium Books, 2012.

This book is a work of fiction. Names, characters, places and incidents are either a product of the author's imagination or are used fictitiously. Any resemblance to actual events, locales or persons, living or dead, is entirely coincidental.

ISBN-13: 978-1499516838
ISBN-10: 1499516835

1

"Hello?" said subject 1 uncertainly, looking all around her as she let herself into the room. It was very small. Had it been a closet at one time? Maybe even a restroom? There were a few holes in the stained linoleum of the floor that plumbing might once have passed through. Now there was only an office chair positioned under a naked light bulb. And the mural.

The mural covered all four walls. She didn't know if it really qualified as a mural, however, wasn't clear on the definition. Did a mural have to portray a certain scene, inhabited by a number of characters? If so, maybe she would simply classify the art as graffiti instead. This graffiti had claimed every inch of the walls, but was cut off neatly at the margins of the ceiling and floor, as if those areas had been masked off while the artist had worked. An odd technique for a vandal.

She closed the door after her, still glancing around. She saw no security camera positioned near the ceiling as she might have expected. No apparent microphone. Those holes in the floor, she decided; a microphone must be secreted in there. Maybe the researcher whose name had sounded like Onsay (and what nationality was that?) was sitting in a room directly below this one, even now. But when she lowered herself into the chair, the holes in the floor were situated behind her. The chair was not turned to face the closed door, either, but one of the graffiti-slathered walls. Subject 1 thought it best not to swivel it in another direction. She gripped its padded armrests nervously.

"Can you hear me?" she spoke aloud self consciously. "Dr. Onsay told us we could come in here any time of day or night, in no particular order. Is that right? Hello?"

No answer. No indication that there was indeed someone listening at all times, or at least that her words were being recorded. Should she continue anyway? Yes, she had to. It was a condition of her contract. Every day she must come in here, just like the others. Not only had she been told she could do so at any time she chose, but she could also discuss any subject matter she chose, whether it be about her nine companions or about her own life. Her past, her present situation, or her dreams for the future.

She had phrased her words just now as if someone other than Dr. Onsay might be monitoring this confession room, but she had only ever seen Dr. Onsay, and only that one time. The initial interview, in a stark little second-floor office in the city. An office that looked as if it had been rented just for a short time, not a picture on its walls of ugly cheap paneling, just Dr. Onsay's laptop resting on the battered gray metal desk.

Laid off from her position as a computer software designer, in her ongoing frustrating job search subject 1 had encountered an ad presumably posted by Dr. Onsay on the classified advertisement site Craigslist, wherein was given a link to another website: http://subject11.webs.com. Curious, 1 had visited this site, though ultimately it gave little more information than the ad did itself. It simply stated that a number of local test subjects were required for a study, the pay being four thousand dollars per individual. She had promptly sent an email to the address given on the website, therein providing her cell phone number, and within mere days Dr. Onsay had phoned her to set up the interview.

The other test subjects had related that they had only ever met Dr. Onsay and no other researchers, also. But surely Onsay couldn't be conducting this experiment alone?

In any case, seated now in the confession chamber, subject 1 had to assume she was indeed being listened to, and not just transmitting her words to her own ears.

"Um…well, I guess I'll just talk, then," she said. "I'll just talk."

Through the narrow lenses of her eyeglasses, with stylish white frames by Roberto Cavalli, she stared at the graffiti mural directly facing her. That was all there was, so this was what she addressed when she spoke.

"Sooo. Okay…I'll tell you about my tattoo." Subject 1 rolled up the right short sleeve of her top. "I have a tramp stamp on my lower back: a Mobius strip in a figure 8, like the symbol for infinity. But this here on my arm – I don't know if you can see it – it says, ONE LIFE TO LIVE. That's a soap opera on TV, and it was always my Mom's favorite. We used to watch it together when I was a kid. Mom had a crush on the character Bo Buchanan, played by Robert S. Woods. Maybe it was because Bo was a Vietnam vet, and my father was in the Marines. He left us when I was only eight, twenty years ago, and I haven't seen him since."

Her words briefly faltered. The graffiti confronting her was beginning to make her eyes hurt. It was like gazing at a giant paisley pattern, all bristling swirling shapes. Except it was all painted in black and white. The words, if they could be called words, teenagers spray-painted on any available city surface – a practice called tagging – always struck her as being symbols from an alien language, like hieroglyphics, and these were no exception. The tagged symbols overlapped each other, some in white and others in black but none of them making any kind of sense to her. The background itself varied from black to white. It was a dizzying chaos and she wanted to look away, but the densely layered graffiti was to either side of her and behind, too.

She'd give them just a little more, just to fulfill the bargain, and then she'd get out of there.

"Last year my Mom died from from uterine cancer. I used to sit with her in the hospital watching *One Life to Live*, just like when I was a kid."

Subject 1's eyes had grown moist, her chin quivering. She tried to clamp down hard on her emotions, just long enough to finish. The chaos of graffiti was making her queasy; she thought she might even be sick to her stomach if she didn't get out of there soon. Could part of it be claustrophobia? The lingering smell of the paint in this poorly ventilated room?

"That's why I got this tattoo," she concluded. "ONE LIFE TO LIVE."

She waited a few beats, but there was no acknowledgement. No voice over a microphone to thank or dismiss her. So, rolling down her sleeve again to cover the tattoo, she rose from her chair and said, "Okay, well I guess that's it. See you tomorrow, then."

Subject 1 opened the door, but turned in the threshold to glance back into the room. The graffiti looked to be swarming upon the walls, like strange organisms under a microscope's lens. She squeezed her eyes tight for several seconds until the worst of her nausea passed. Then, reopening her eyes, she stepped out of the confessional and pulled the door shut after her, quickly, lest her gaze became lost in those disorienting, seething walls again.

2

They each had to take six different pills every morning. These pills were already portioned out and sealed in a white envelope, and these envelopes came down a thick PVC pipe that pierced through the ceiling, to drop into a plastic bucket. Every morning they would find ten envelopes in the bucket, each with a number printed on it in pencil. Ten paper lunch bags, stapled shut, would also drop into the bucket every morning. Inside the lunch bags were an apple, a banana, and a cereal bar with raspberry filling. The lunch bags had numbers penciled on them, too. They could drink all the water they wanted from a sink in this room, though the water tasted faintly of fluoride and rust.

5 opened her lunch bag and complained, "My cereal bar is smooshed."

"My apple is dented," 6 noted.

"My vitamin is broken," 2 observed.

"What makes you think that's a vitamin?" asked 10.

4 shifted the tall white bucket to one side, knelt down on the floor and tried peering up through the end of the PVC pipe affixed to the wall with metal bands. "Too dark," he reported. He removed his eye from the hole and positioned his mouth beneath it instead. "Hallooo!" he called.

The others were already beginning to seat themselves around a long table with metal legs and a Formica top with a speckled granite design. There were five chairs to either side, with metal frames and torn vinyl seats showing the spongy padding inside. The rustling and tearing of envelopes and lunch bags. 8 balled up his lunch bag and tossed it toward the plastic bucket as if launching a basketball at a hoop. It bounced off the rim. "Ohh!" he exclaimed.

"Why even write our numbers on the envelopes?" 9 groused, lining up her pills in a neat row before her. "We all get exactly the same stuff."

"Looks that way," 10 replied. "But we don't know that's true."

9 lifted her gaze to stare across at him. "I hadn't thought of that."

"We don't even know if they do something to the food," 7 said, but she then took a large crunching bite out of her apple.

They had already filled their ten plastic tumblers with water from the oversized metal sink jutting from one wall of the nearly empty chamber – which was long and wide, with a high ceiling of exposed metal beams and joists, walls tiled with white glazed bricks, and huge windows comprised of many small panes, most filmed over as if with cataracts. The ten of them had quickly developed their own system for ensuring that they all swallowed the six pills, as mandated by their initial instructions. First the five people on one side of the table swallowed pill after pill, one at a time, observed by the person seated directly opposite. Then it was the turn of the five people on the other side of the table.

There was one large yellow-brown tablet that looked like a vitamin. 1 had commented that it tasted like a vitamin, too, and made her urine yellow like the vitamins she took every day at home. There was one very small white pill. There was a two-piece gel capsule that looked like an antibiotic, half red and half white. There was a slightly smaller time release capsule, half green and half white. And there were two identical one-piece gel capsules of a very attractive green color; 1 had said they looked like bath oil beads.

3 started choking; the yellow-brown tablet, the biggest of the pills, had stuck in her throat. To her right, 4 pushed at 3's hand to urge her to drink more water. On 3's left, 2 began thumping her on the back. With a deep retch, 3 coughed the pill back into her hand, her eyes tearing. The pill's coating was already dissolving, staining her palm yellow. Hoarsely, she said, "Fuck," but she immediately popped the tablet into her mouth again, tossed back her head and took more gulping swallows of water. This time she got the pill down successfully.

"You okay?" asked 2, rubbing her back with a large hand.

"I hate swallowing pills," she told him. "Next time I should break that one in half."

"I wish I'd given you my vitamin," 2 said. "It was broken."

It had been their own idea to seat themselves in numerical order at every meal, but their numbers had already been designated for them at the beginning. They had been very firmly instructed not to reveal their true names.

They had no cell phones, no wristwatches, and there were no clocks on the walls. They only knew from the changing of day to night and night to day, outside the derelict building's windows, that this was their third breakfast together.

**

9 and 10 had been conversing in one of the building's many long corridors, the paint on its walls extensively flaking off like the decomposing skin of a great creature, but they stopped when they heard a rhythmic clapping sound, growing louder as it approached. The clapping became accompanied by huffing animal-like pants. They stepped back, to opposite sides of the corridor, to let 4 dart between them. They turned to watch him as he continued jogging off down the hallway, until he took a corner and the slapping of his sneakers receded.

"Do you think one of us isn't really a subject, but one of the testers observing us up close?" 9 asked 10.

"Maybe only one of us is the subject," 10 said, "and the rest of us are all testers."

9 looked at 10 with a new kind of wariness, and slowly replied, "I hadn't thought of that."

One wall of the corridor was lined with a row of barred windows, and 10 leaned close to the nearest of them. A corner of the window was broken, and glass fragments ground against each other under his sneakers. Through the dirty panes he scanned the building's grounds, overgrown with tall leeched grass, rampant weeds like great clumps of steel wool, autumn leaves that drifted and swirled in chilly gusts he could feel through the gap in the glass. Other buildings to the sides and across the way appeared to be part of this complex, but were they distinct structures or all one connected, sprawling mass? It only being the third day, and without having explored too extensively, he hadn't formed a map of the layout in his mind.

"These bars are new," 10 stated. "Look at them. The paint is shiny…it isn't chipped. They're not rusted. I'm sure they're new."

"I don't know – why go through all the trouble of

putting bars on so many windows? Maybe this was a prison, or a crazy hospital."

"There are no cells that I've seen, for a prison. And no hospital beds for a hospital."

"The place is stripped to a shell," 9 persisted. "There could have been beds."

"There aren't a lot of small rooms like you'd expect to see in any kind of hospital. Just big rooms, mostly."

"The big rooms could have been open wards. What do you think this place was?"

"I don't know. Factory of some kind, I'd guess."

"A factory with bars on the windows?"

"That's what I'm saying; they added the bars for our experiment."

"Come on – they couldn't find a place that already had bars on the windows, or a smaller place at least if they needed to do that? And anyway, why bars? We're volunteers, not prisoners."

10 turned from the window to face her again. "So far, we aren't," he said, as if to tease her. But if he meant to playfully make her nervous, he kept a straight face about it.

9 shivered, and rubbed her arms against the breeze wafting in through the corridor's long row of partially shattered windows. Glancing at the window 10 had just peered through, she complained, "God, it's cold in here. And what's with the fall leaves out there? It's still summer."

**

2 and 3 explored another corridor, built from cinderblock. There were no windows here, but fluorescent lights overhead provided illumination. This unhealthy glow made the glossy white paint of the walls glisten wetly, but the paint was in fact webbed with cracks and blistered.

As they walked side by side, 3 was so tiny she didn't even come to 2's shoulder. He was tall, thick-bodied, with a neat gelled haircut, his beefy face clean-shaven but with shaded jowls. He wore white hospital scrubs. They all did. The petite and gamine-faced 3 had mid-length, coal black hair and caramel skin.

Glancing down at her as they strolled, 2 grinned and said, "So what nationality are you?"

"You can't ask me that."

"What? Oh no, nobody said we couldn't talk about personal stuff, as long as we don't give our names, addresses, details like that. I'm sure they want us to chitchat so they can see how we interact. After all, look what the experiment is about. 'Social integration,' Dr. Onsay said."

"Do you think there are cameras?"

"Oh," 2 said, flicking his eyes this way and that, "I'm sure of it." His gaze returned to his companion. "So what nationality are you? Filipino? Thai?"

"Irish."

"Irish. Riiight. Me, I'm an Eskimo."

"You look Italian. You look like an Italian cop. Or a mafia guy."

"Hoo-boy," 2 chuckled. "You see right through me, huh? Truth is I'm a cop but I moonlight as a mafia guy on weekends. No, seriously, do you want me to tell you what I do?"

"I'm sure that's against the rules."

"Whatever. How 'bout telling me how old you are, at least? I'm thirty-four."

"I'm thirty-eight."

"What?" He stopped in his tracks. "Get out! Come on, now."

She beamed bright teeth, pleased by his reaction. "It's true. Maybe I look young to you because I'm small."

"Well it isn't just that – it's your face, everything. You're so cute, you look twenty-something. I can't believe you're older than me."

"I am."

"Do you have kids?"

"You mean, am I married?" Looking away from him but still smiling knowingly, 3 resumed walking.

"Well…"

"Divorced. One kid: Tania. She's with my husband right now, so I can do this. How about you?"

"Same and same. Divorced, but mine's a son – Nathan – and he's with his mom." 2 wagged a finger at her. "Hey, if you're divorced you can't call your ex your husband."

3 shrugged. "Habit."

"Is he the same nationality as you?"

"White, like you."

"So he's a mafia guy, too?"

"An Eskimo mafia guy."

"Oh! They're badass. One wrong move, you wake up with a seal's head at the foot of your bed."

**

In the confessional, on the ground floor and just off the great room that served as their banquet hall, 5 had decided to get her daily monologue out of the way. Outside, 7 waited her turn, after which they had agreed to widen their exploration of the facility together. As 5 explained to the mural she faced: "I think that's part of the experiment; you're waiting to see which of us will be timid or lazy and stick close to our quarters, and which of us will be more daring or curious and want to explore. Maybe you want to see if we'll follow an instinct to find a way to escape, even though we're not prisoners."

5 pivoted in the padded office chair, from one side to the other, surveying the explosive splashes of black and white graffiti, like an entire galaxy of stars all gone supernova at the same time, spattering their glowing fire and dark matter in every direction. As she did so she continued speaking. "It's natural that we're pairing off. I'm sure you want to see how that breaks down. Of course some guys and girls are bonding. Me and 7 hit it off right away. Maybe she's not interested in finding a boyfriend, even a temporary one…same as me.

"I already have my Seth. He works with me in the pharmaceutical company I mentioned in my interview. I have more vacation time than he does, so I figured why not do this, and get paid for it by you and my company at the same time, huh?

"I miss him already. I hope he's missing me. Sometimes…well, sometimes I get the feeling he wouldn't miss me if I just upped and disappeared. But that's a story for another day. Or a bunch of days.

"Anyway," 5 said, waving away her digression, "the pattern here is obvious, especially when we sit down to eat. I'm 5 and female, and 7 is female. So sure enough, 1, 3 and 9 are female, and 2, 4, 6, 8 and 10 are male. Does that mean women are always perceived as odd? Heh. I'm sure it's just an arbitrary way to do it.

"No one is very young, and nobody's old. I'd say 7 is the youngest; she told me she's twenty. 10 looks the oldest. He hasn't said, but I'd say he's at least forty.

"Do I win a prize for my observations? Does that make me a star guinea pig? If you want to reward me, how about some bottled water? The water from the sink is gross. I can't believe we have to drink that. Aren't you afraid we might get sick from old chemicals or whatever that might be in the system?

"Speaking of chemicals – like I say, I work for a pharmaceutical company, in the R & D department." She smiled. "I don't know what these meds are that you've got us taking every morning, whether they're the basis of the test or just something in support of the test, but…" she wagged a scolding finger in the air "…I can tell you, if this is a drug trial it's not the way the FDA would want to see it done."

5 rose from the chair and stretched, deciding she'd given them enough for today, and itching to get to exploring with 7. Before she opened the door, looking up at the blank ceiling as if an eye might be peeking through a crack in the plaster, she said, "And maybe there's something funny in the water that you *want* us to drink."

She put her hand on the doorknob, but as an afterthought turned back to address the room again in a low, confidential voice. "Actually, I get the vibe that 7 might be a lesbian, or at least bisexual, but that's okay. I'm not prejudiced, and I don't feel threatened – I'm secure in who I am."

**

"Well, will you look at this," said 2, as he and 3 turned into a corridor they hadn't encountered before.

He had the impression they had passed out of one building in the complex and into another, older section – maybe the original body from which the other had sprouted over time. The walls of this corridor were composed of bare ruddy brick, not plaster or cinderblock, and the windows lining one wall were narrow like those of a castle tower, arched at the tops. They apparently didn't require bars, being made up of small panes set in a metal web, like the huge windows in the banquet hall. The floor here was of wood, having lost its sheen of varnish, the boards squeaking under their weight. The ceiling of wooden beams and exposed pipes was festooned with sooty cobwebs.

But more striking than the red brick and worn wooden floorboards was the mural that entirely filled the wall opposite to the one lined with windows. Like the mural in the confessional, the paint had not encroached on the floor or ceiling, though it covered every inch of the bricks along this length of wall. It was identical in style to the graffiti mural in the confessional. Riotous splashes of black and white formed a background for a crazy interplay of tagging. Skeletal scribbles and jagged scrawls like mutant fish bones, or else bloated balloon words like amorphous bulging amebas. Taken as a whole, the mural oddly called to mind for 2 an apocalyptic landscape, the tagging like rolls of concertina wire overlapping shattered fences and exploded ruins burnt to cinders.

Like clouds trawling across the sky, or the blotted ink of a Rorschach test, 2 imagined you could read what you wanted into the mural. Focusing more on its particulars, rather than the whole, he felt he recognized some of these odd symbols from the confessional's walls.

"I don't know if this stuff was done by kids who broke in here over the years," he said to 3, "or if it's some kind of intentional decoration, put here by the owners."

"It can't be too old, because it smells fresh," 3 said. "All I know is it's ugly – like that Jackson Pollock shit."

"I was thinking more like Picasso's *Guernica*," 2 said. "On acid." He scrutinized the mural some more, and muttered as if only speaking to himself, "It's almost cosmic. It sort of looks like the Big Bang. The start of creation."

3

On the fourth day, during their second of three daily meals, 2 said to the group, "This is getting to be cruel and unusual punishment. I didn't figure we'd have to go without coffee. I'm a big-time coffee addict, and I'm getting withdrawal headaches."

"Coffee?" said 10. "How do you think I feel? I'd strangle a puppy for a cigarette right about now."

7 was watching as 1 gave 6 her bologna sandwich in return for his orange and a sandwich bag full of grapes. She spoke up, "You know, you really shouldn't be trading food."

1 looked back at her icily through the narrow lenses of her glasses. "I'm a vegetarian."

"I think the idea here is we all eat the same."

"And why would that be?"

"I don't know – in case the food is drugged or whatever."

"In case the food is drugged? I don't think they need to trick us into taking drugs; we do it willingly every morning. And if it is drugged, then I'll eat some extra drugged fruit and he can eat some extra drugged bologna. I'm a vegetarian and I'm not eating meat; too bad. This is between 6 and me."

"Whatever…I'm just saying."

To divert the conversation from hostility, 5 cut in,

"Yesterday 7 and I were exploring for hours and we saw some interesting things."

"Like what?" 6 asked around a mouthful of sandwich.

"Well, we worked our way all the way around to those buildings opposite this one – you know, that you can see outside the windows here?" She gestured across the room toward the looming windows with their small cloudy panes. They projected golden afternoon light across the floor in a grid like a giant chessboard.

"So the buildings are all connected," 10 said. "Or did you get outside?"

"No – just for the hell of it we tried every door to the outside we found. They're all locked. Anyway, the last building we poked around in is in rough shape – really old. Must have been derelict long before this one got retired. The walls are all damp and black from mildew. Nasty. Where the plaster is broken away you can see the bricks underneath, and some of the floors feel like they're going to collapse right under your feet."

"But tell them what we found over there," 7 urged her.

"In one room with a couple empty file cabinets and an empty desk, there was a big wooden table or maybe it was a workbench – and it had doll heads on it. Doll heads all lined up, standing on their necks. Some were small like Barbie heads, and some were old baby doll heads, made of cracked rubber. Very weird."

"Ah, kids have got in here over the years," 8 said dismissively.

"There were ten doll heads," 5 said, holding his gaze with an intense expression. "I counted them."

"Okay…ten doll heads. Big deal."

"Five were lined up on one side of the table, facing five heads on the other side. Just like we're sitting now."

"Oh wow," 9 said, and she hugged herself with a

visible shudder.

"Oh, one of us here must have done it as a joke." 4 grinned around the table at his companions. "Fess up, one of you!"

"Could have been Dr. Onsay," 2 suggested, "or some other tester. Maybe they have a camera set up and were just waiting for us to find that."

"It's nothing," 8 said. "Kids. Just kids."

"Tell them the other thing we found over there," 7 said.

5 resumed, "In that same really rundown building, we found stairs going down into a basement. Believe it or not there were lights on here and there, just like on this side, so we decided to go down and have a look. There wasn't much down there; just a lot of big old water pipes on the walls or the ceiling. But we did find one funny thing in the basement, in this narrow little dungeon-looking corridor with an arched ceiling. It was more of that same graffiti like in our confessional." She nodded at the closed door across the room. "Covering one whole wall."

"Really?" 1 said. "God, what is it with that graffiti, anyway?"

8 barked a laugh. "What's up with graffiti? It's just fucking kids! Come on!"

1 turned to him. "Don't you feel funny when you're in the confessional? Doesn't staring at that graffiti too long make you feel dizzy?"

8 grinned at her and said, "No. But staring at you too long makes me dizzy." He winked.

"Oh please."

2 turned to look at 3, seated beside him. "Hey, you wanna go over there and have a look after we eat?"

"Huh? To see doll heads and more graffiti? I don't think so." The small, attractive woman detected the disappointment and embarrassment in 2's face and nudged him with her elbow. "Let's just take a walk around here in this building, where it isn't moldy at least."

2 brightened. "Yeah, maybe you're right. Those heads could've been left by my rival mafia," he joked. "As a warning to me."

"Don't worry – I'll protect you."

8 had overheard their plans and, still grinning, said, "Hey, I want to go with you two. You trying to hog that pretty little lady all to yourself, Mr. 2?"

2 glared across the table at the other man, who wore wire-rimmed glasses and a full beard as if to compensate for his fine, receding hair. "I'm not stopping you. But I'm not inviting you, either. Ever heard the expression three's a crowd?"

"Don't you think it should be up to the lady if somebody wants to hang out with her?"

3 twisted her full lips in a pouty sneer and said, "Do whatever you want – it's a free country."

"Jeesh…okay then, forget it. I can see when I'm not wanted. Maybe you two can find a bed in your travels."

2 stood up so abruptly that his tumbler of water tipped over. He pointed at the other man and snarled, "Watch your mouth, asshole!"

"Okay, whew, take it easy!"

4 had risen from his seat as well, and put his hand on 2's arm. "Be cool, man, he's just fuckin' around a little."

"I don't need to hear that shit." 2 slowly sank back into his chair.

7 leaned close to 5 and whispered, "They're watching this, I'm sure. They love it – it's what they're counting on. It won't be interesting for them if we don't go for each other's throats."

***

"It's spooky out there," 9 said, still hugging her arms as she stood at a barred window, peering out into the crisp blackness of night. Distantly, tiny yellow windows glowed as if floating in the inky air. They were windows in the older building across the way; the building 5 and 7 had explored the day before.

Several of the test subjects were doing their laundry in a room in which a modern washer and dryer had been set up for them. At the start of the experiment, they had each been given one extra pair of white hospital scrubs. While the washer and dryer churned, the sound of spraying water came from another chamber beyond. This was one of two shower rooms that had been prepared for them, both containing no more than a flexible hand shower attached to a faucet, with a drain in the tiled floor. No bath tub, no shower curtain, not even a door in the room's threshold. One shower room was used by the women, the other by the men, and as there was but a single shower hose in each room the subjects had taken to showering at different times of the day to avoid waiting in a line. Some of them had protested at the coldness of the water, or at this mode of showering altogether, but 3 had said, "This is how I always showered back in my country."

"And what country is that?" 7 had asked her, but as if she regretted her words, 3 had not answered.

The sound of spraying water ceased, and moments later 1 stepped into the laundry area, wrapped in one of the two white towels she'd been given and drying her hair with the other. 9 turned toward the females' shower room to take her place, while 1 slapped barefoot into another, larger room. Here, the cinderblock walls had been painted halfway up from the floor in a dull red color like old dried blood. This was the females' sleeping room. 1 went to where her sleeping bag was rolled up. Some of the others left their sleeping bags spread open on the floor all the time, but 1 was afraid of bugs or even mice stealing inside.

She was changing into her clean set of scrubs when she looked up and saw that young 7 had trailed into the room after her, and was watching her as she removed her towel, revealing her still damp body. "Is something wrong?" 1 asked sharply.

"No…sorry…I was, um, just reading your tattoo, there. ONE LIFE TO LIVE."

"Oh. Yeah."

"I have a philosophical tattoo, myself. Here." 7 turned around and lifted her top with one hand, pulling down the back of her pants with the other, to reveal a tattoo nestled in the small of her back. In flowery, scrolling type surrounded by sparkles were the words LIFE'S NO STORYBOOK.

"Cute," 1 said. But she didn't show her own lower back tattoo, of a Mobius strip. She donned her clothing as quickly as possible.

Looking elsewhere awkwardly, 7 stammered, "I like your glasses…they're cool."

"Thanks."

"Um…so you're a vegetarian, huh?"

"My Mom died of cancer. I try to live healthy to avoid the same fate."

"Oh man…I'm sorry about that."

Glancing toward the young woman as she straightened the hem of her top, and feeling a little guilty for her snappy tone, 1 said, "So you found more of that graffiti, huh?"

"Yeah." 7 took this as an invitation to face her. "That makes three places I know of in this facility, including the confessional."

"The confessional! Shit!"

"What's wrong?"

"Usually I do my confession early, but today I put it off…and then I forgot about it altogether."

"Oh wow. Well you'd better go do it now, then. I'm sure they keep track of these things. It's what we're getting paid for."

1 looked toward the doorway to the sleeping quarters dubiously. Reluctantly. "Yeah, I know."

"What's wrong? You afraid to go over there alone? It's just a couple rooms over. I can go with you, and wait in the cafeteria if you want."

1 was still uncomfortable with the young woman's attentions, remembering how she had seemed to be staring at her exposed body. "No, that's okay," she said. She slipped on her stylish glasses with their white frames. "I can go alone. Like you said, it's not far…and I'll only give them a couple minutes, just to make it look good."

***

"10 and I were trying to figure out what this place was," 9 said to the wall in the closed confession room. "He says factory, but I was thinking hospital or prison. I didn't tell him I've worked in real estate. Or that I wasn't much good at it. Had the smarts, but just not aggressive enough. *Anyway*, to be honest his guess is as good as mine. I never exactly sold abandoned…whatever this property was, before. I'm curious how much you paid to rent it."

Restless in her chair, she knotted her hands between her legs as if in secret prayer. "But I don't know – now I'm feeling sorry I ever agreed to this. It's really not enough money to be living like this, even for a short time. Drinking rusty water, showering in rusty water, living in this place that's probably full of toxic waste, with these...*people.*

"I'm not even sure what the point of it all is. Today 10 said Dr. Onsay told him it was a study in 'social integration.' I said Dr. Onsay told me it was a study of 'temporal distortion.' I'm sure that's what he said. 10 just laughed and said, 'That doesn't make any sense.' Then he thought about what I said and he asked me, 'Did you say *he*?' And I said, 'What?' And he said, 'Talking about Dr. Onsay, did you call her a *he*?' And I said, '*Her*? What do you mean, *her*? Yes, Dr. Onsay is a man.' And 10 said, 'Well, I guess I can see how you might think that. She's definitely on the masculine side. But the person who interviewed me was a woman.' And I said, 'Well, he was definitely gay, but he was definitely a man.' Maybe it wasn't even the same person. Maybe there are a number of different people working on this project, and they're all using the same fake name."

9 yawned, and went on, "But you know who you are, right Dr. Onsay?" She was about to rise from the office chair and go seek out her sleeping bag, when she settled her weight again and said, "Oh...right before I came in here I was finishing up my clothes and towels in the laundry, when I looked out the window in there and I saw someone standing in one of the lit windows in that old building 5 was talking about at lunch. It was just an outline, but it was definitely a person looking back over this way. It gave me the creeps, because it felt like they were looking at me, too. It was probably one of our team, gone over there to poke around. But it might have been you, too, huh Dr. Onsay? Right? Could've been you – or one of you."

4

"What I wouldn't give for some *music*," 7 told the close walls of the confessional. "Or a TV. Or just to check my email. God – you couldn't let us have one laptop we could share? When I signed up, I didn't really stop to think about the stuff I'd miss. The things I rely on.

"I miss weed, too, but I guess that's too much to ask." She snorted. "At least I'm thankful you give us soap, toothpaste and toilet paper, so I don't feel like a *total* savage.

"Another thing I really miss about not having a computer is being able to work on my art. I'm a pretty damn good artist, I'll have you know; I'll be going back to school in the fall. Most of my stuff is done on the computer, but I wish I at least had a sketchbook with me. The boredom here will kill me. By the way, that's some pretty wild graffiti we're seeing around – was that stuff already here before you rented the place? And those doll heads we found; it reminds me of an art project I did in high school, where I made a baby's crib mobile out of doll heads."

7 paused to release a great sigh, then resumed, "Well, frankly I've been masturbating like crazy to take the edge off my stress. I lie down between 5 and 9 every night. I don't mean snuggled between them – though that would ne nice – but it still makes me feel kind of…you know. I feel

closest to 5, but 9 is more attractive. She must be almost forty, but she's still hot. The guys seem most attracted to 3 – I can feel these things – but I don't see it myself. She just seems dirty to me. I don't mean because she's an Asian or whatever she is, I just mean…I don't know. I just don't like her vibe, like she's really this sleazy conniving little bitch who comes across as all cute and shit. She acts as though she doesn't like the guys checking her out, but you know she really thrives on it. She must bring out their inner pedophile, because she's so teeny. Maybe she brings out their inner bisexual, too, because she's built like a little boy, and she has this pretty little boy face. Not my kind of woman.

"And none of the guys appeal to me. As usual with guys, they're either assholes – like 8 and 10 – or boring, like 2 and 4. I haven't figured out which type the black guy, 6, is…but he is the youngest, so if I had to choose I'd go with him. But I choose not to choose. Anyway, today I saw 6 talking with 3 at the mess hall table, when they were the only ones in the room until I came in, and 6 was holding her hand while they talked, but he let go and they looked all embarrassed when they saw me. Christ. She's gotta be ten years older than him, but he must have Asianitis, too. Then later, I saw 2 looking for 3…he was asking people if they knew where she was. He asked me, too, and I said I didn't know. It was a pitiful sight indeed. He was like a big stupid dog whose master has left him home alone. I didn't mention to 2, so I don't know if he realized it himself, that 6 wasn't around either.

"So…unless you people want to bring in some much cooler guys than these, I'll maintain my secret crushes on 5 and 9. 5's waiting for me outside right now; after I'm done in here we'll be doing some more exploring. We're going to see if there's anything interesting on the upper floors of that moldy old brick building. Heh…maybe she'll get spooked over there and hug me, and I can comfort her."

****

"So where did you disappear to?" 2 asked 3 as they set out walking together, on what had become their daily stroll. They were later than usual, today.

"I just needed to be alone for a little while, to think about some things."

"Was I one of the things you were thinking about?" He made it sound like a joke.

She smiled mysteriously and shrugged, without looking up at him. "Maybe."

After a short while they stepped into a stairwell that echoed hollowly with their movement and voices. 2 and 3 leaned over its blistered metal rail to peek below. A basement level? There were no lights on down there, so they might as well have been gazing into an infinite abyss. Standing very close to 3, 2 made an exaggerated show of sniffing at the air and said, "We're all using the same bars of soap and the same laundry detergent…so how is it that you smell better than everyone else?"

3 shrugged again. "Some people just have a natural good odor."

"I've read that odor plays a big part in people's attraction to each other, on a subliminal level."

"But some people just have a bad odor, too. Like 4. Have you ever smelled him up close?"

"No. Have you ever smelled him up close?"

3 smiled at him, and bumped him with her elbow. "Are you jealous?"

"Maybe."

"No, I don't have to get close to him…his odor is

strong enough. But I think it's because he's always jogging through the buildings."

2 took her arm and pulled her back away from the railing. "Come on, let's not lean on that too much; you never know if it'll give way and you and me will take a nosedive." He didn't let go of her arm, however, and she turned to face him, raising her full dark eyebrows inquisitively. 2's words stumbled over each other's feet. "Hey look…I know you don't want to tell me your name or where you live or anything because of the test, but after this I really want to see you again. I mean, see you seriously. You said you're divorced, and I told you I'm divorced, and I don't care at all that you have a child already, so long as you don't care that I have one. I know you don't want to hear my particulars either, but I'll tell you this much: I have a good job. I can take care of you and your kid."

3 smiled. "The mafia pays well, huh?"

"Sure does."

"If you have a good job, why are you free to do this experiment? You must need the money."

"Okay, I'll tell you. I'm a school teacher. And it's summer."

"School teacher? Wow. I was wrong about you. And that's a good job?"

"Well…"

"It's so early to talk like this, don't you think? It hasn't even been a week."

"I don't want to wait for somebody else to scoop you up." Again, he made it sound like a joke, but his words were actually very straightforward.

"Who's going to scoop me up? Someone in here?"

"Here, there, or anywhere."

"But you don't really know me."

"I know in my guts that I know enough."

"Maybe I don't know enough."

"Okay. So after this is over, give me a chance and you can get to know me."

She slipped out of his hand, but was still smiling. "We'll see." She gestured toward another flight of cement stairs that proceeded through the ceiling to a second floor. "Come on…let's go see what's up there."

2 agreed. For now he had to be content with the fact that she still desired his company, and was willing to continue in their directionless journey together.

****

"You okay?" 4 asked 5, outside the closed door of the confession room.

5 turned to face him. Her eyes had been shut, and she still held a hand pressed to her brow. "What?" she asked in a slurred, disoriented voice.

"Do you have a headache?"

"Um…I feel kind of nauseous, actually. I almost passed out for a second there, I think."

"You all right now? Maybe you'd better sit down."

"Yeah. I was going to do some more exploring today, but think I'd better go lie down a little more. I didn't really sleep well last night. Crazy dreams, or whatever."

"I think you should." 4 motioned toward the closed door. "You waiting for someone?"

5 regarded the door, blinking in bewilderment. "Um. I, ah…I don't think so. No."

"Do you need to make your confession?"

"No, I already did." 5 stepped to one side. "Be my guest."

"Go lie down, will ya?"

"I will."

4 rapped on the door, waited a few ticks, then rapped again. "Hello?" He turned the knob, opened the door. The confessional was empty. He slipped inside and shut the door after him.

5 lingered for a few moments, staring at the door, then turned away to seek out her sleeping bag in the women's makeshift dormitory.

****

"There they are." 10 moved forward to the scarred old wooden work table, where a varied mix of doll heads in two rows had been assembled to confront each other. 9 hung back a bit, as if the sight of them were too disturbing. 10 examined them more closely, and reported, "Yep – eight of them, just like 5 said."

"Eight?" 9's tone was puzzled.

10 looked over his shoulder at her. "Yeah. Why?"

9 shook her head. "Nothing. So…okay, eight doll heads. Must have been kids messing around in here, like 8 said."

"Perhaps." 10 lifted each doll head in turn, peering into its hollow skull through its open neck stump. "Nothing hidden inside. Rats…I thought there might be a clue or something. A key to open a locked section of the complex, or a key to get outside. I thought maybe they were challenging our puzzle-solving abilities. That would be more fun, wouldn't it?"

"We're not inside a video game."

10 peeked into the final doll head, its scalp just a pink hemisphere perforated with holes, and one blue eye missing. "Lobotomy complete," he remarked as he set it back down. "Come on, let's go find that graffiti they were

talking about."

"Why?"

"It's just funny, that's all. You have something better to do? You can always go back to camp on your own, if you want." He smirked.

"On my own? Thanks a lot. I'll come with you."

****

"I'm nothing too out of the ordinary," 4 said, in between biting his nails and spitting little shreds of them onto the floor of the closet-like room that served as the confessional. "I don't know if that's good or bad for your study. I guess if there was one unusual thing to define me, it would be…" He stopped short. Spit out a crescent sliver of nail, slick with his saliva. It looked to him like it got stuck on the glossy, graffiti-coated wall. "It would be that I was molested by a priest when I was eleven. Good old Father Ryan. He's dead now – may he burn in Hell. Yeah…that's sad, huh, if that's the most outstanding thing that's ever happened in my life?

"Well, I guess I'm not even really out of the ordinary in that sense, either. It's not like a lot of boys haven't been molested that way. I was reading about one fucker in Wisconsin who molested two hundred deaf boys. Nice, huh? Who knows what issues they might have had to deal with, since. Not bad enough being deaf, right? But I guess we're all scarred in some way. Fractured and incomplete.

"Can I truly blame that for the failings of my life? The failings of all my relationships? The disappointments in my career? Or am I just making excuses, and not taking enough responsibility for my own actions – or inactions?

"My ex-girlfriend Hanna told me something once. It struck me as being a lot of facile psychological bullshit at the time, but who knows? It might be true. When we were fighting a short time before we broke up, she said, 'You know why you like to jog? Because you only understand running. That's all you do. Run away. But you don't know what from...and you don't know where to.'"

****

3 had begun climbing the stairs ahead of 2. Ascending behind her, he had taken advantage of this arrangement to watch the movements of her bottom in her white scrub pants. She reached the second floor landing ahead of him, took several steps, and cried out.

"What? What is it?" 2 said, quickening his pace up the remaining cement steps. Was she swatting at a hornet?

3 was batting at the air around her head as she turned in jerky circles, quickly switched to tousling her black hair. "Oh God...check me for a spider! Look at my back, quick!"

"Okay, okay, hold still a second." He took hold of her shoulders.

"Look in my hair! I felt it in my hair!" She rubbed her hands across her face vigorously. "As soon as I came up here I walked right through a spider web. God – I hate spiders!"

He ran his hands through her hair, then brushed off her shoulders, back, and the outside of her arms. He felt guilty for enjoying this excuse to touch her, in the face of her distress. "I'm not seeing anything...not even webs. Are you sure one of your own hairs didn't blow across your face?"

"I know the difference." 3 tilted her head back, and pointed at the ceiling near the area where the staircase continued on up to a third level. "Hey, you see that?"

2 followed her finger. An inky stain had spread across the ceiling. From it, a few attenuated strands dangled like dripping glue. Simultaneously, the two of them dropped their gaze to the floor at their feet. A few similar black splatters. 2 scuffed at one of these with the toe of his sneaker, but the stain here had dried. "Yeah, maybe a few strings of this gummy stuff were hanging down. Roof tar, or something?"

3 felt at her hair again. "Maybe. Let's go see."

This time, 2 took the lead up the stairs, toward the third floor.

****

"And here we are," 10 said. "5 was right – it does look like something out of a dungeon."

Ahead of him and 9 was the mouth of a narrow, brick-lined basement hallway, with a curved ceiling that made it appear more like an antiquated sewer tunnel. Even outside the corridor's entrance, they could see the graffiti that covered the whole of the right-hand wall.

10 observed, "I wonder if this building goes back to the nineteenth cent–"

But his words were sliced away. From beyond the far end of the hallway, they'd heard a single shrill cry. It echoed toward them down the length of the corridor. To that point in his life, 10 had never experienced the sensation that authors so readily described, of the hairs rising on the back of one's neck. At that moment, he learned that it was an actual phenomenon.

"Oh my God," 9 moaned, and even as the utterance left her lips, she and 10 saw a figure dart past the end of the brick corridor, from right to left. Just an indistinct silhouette, like a moving smudge, gone in a flicker.

"Fuck," 10 hissed, angry for being startled again so soon. "Who is that?" he bellowed, his voice also amplified by the tunnel. "Who's there? Are you okay? You'd better not be playing fucking games!"

"Let's go," 9 pleaded, pulling at his arm. "Let's get out of here!"

"I can't," he told her, not taking his eyes off the hallway lest the figure reappear. "It might just be some kids fucking around, but it could be somebody in trouble. A homeless person…or one of our own. Come on."

"No, please! Don't you understand?" She tugged at him more insistently. "It isn't one of us, and it isn't a homeless person! It was a *ghost!*"

****

Just off the third floor landing was a hallway. While sunlight beamed in through one large barred window near the stairwell, the hallway itself was in such darkness that it might go on for miles for all that 2 and 3 could tell. Still, enough sunlight touched the start of the hallway for them to see that its entire right-hand wall was plastered with more of the now familiar black and white graffiti.

"Look," 3 said, pointing at the floor beyond the threshold. A glossy black puddle had spread from the base of the graffiti-obscured wall. "That's what it is. The paint was running, and it must have leaked through a crack in the floor."

2 approached the entrance to the corridor, knelt down and poked at the puddle with a finger. Dry, but tacky. He pulled nearly invisible strands of the material between fingertip and thumb. Turning his gaze to the graffiti itself, he saw a design at eye level, white on a field of black: a sideways figure 8 that appeared like the symbol for infinity.

Up close like this, there was a strange quality to the paint that he couldn't quite process, and the murkiness of the hallway wasn't helping. He drew in closer, then closer, until his nose almost touched the wall. The paint had an odd odor, unless that was the wall itself in its state of decay. And then, the paint's unusual quality became clear to him.

At first he had thought the rough texture of the cinderblocks was what lent the paint a kind of grainy appearance. Now he realized the minutely broken aspect to the painted surfaces had another explanation. What at a distance appeared as solid white areas of paint were actually thousands upon thousands of tiny white numbers. And what appeared as solid areas of black paint were comprised of thousands and thousands of nearly microscopic black numbers. Even the background fields of black and white consisted of the same. But whether in black or white paint, there were only two numbers in varying, indecipherable patterns, and those numbers were 0 and 1.

"Binary numbers," 2 mumbled to himself. "Like a code."

As he had indicated to 3, he was a school teacher. He was in fact a math teacher. And so he thought of logic gates and Boolian functions. He thought of ancient binary systems used in Africa for divination, and in Europe for geomancy. He thought, of course, of the use of binary numerals in computers. But he couldn't understand what the artist was trying to express by utilizing them here.

He sat back on his haunches to view the graffiti mural more as a whole again; as much of it as he could make out in the gloom, at least. Fat, blocky balloon words. Spiky, squiggly gang-like tagging. These symbols, names, initials appeared like spontaneous, quickly-rendered blasts from a spay can. Instead, they were intricately composed of numbers the way a painting by Seurat was composed of dots of color. Pixel-like particles, like the cells of an organic body. Not truly graffiti, then, but an artwork of such obsessive detail that it seemed an impossibility to him. His mind spun its wheels in attempting to assimilate it. He wasn't an artist; was there a means of creating such an effect more easily than what he was envisioning? Some kind of stencil, or overlay, or…

"What is it?" 3 asked him. "What do you see?"

He didn't know how to digest it himself, let alone put it into words for another person. And did it really matter, anyway? Why should it seem of such importance? Why should he feel a frost collecting in the core of his bones?

2 rose, and turned to face her. "It's nothing. I'm sure that's what you walked through – a couple goopy strands of this paint, that seeped through the floor." He took her arm. "Come on…let's get back to camp."

5

"Guess I'm the token black guy in the mix, huh?" 6 said as he swiveled the office chair from side to side, tapping his hands on the armrests. "And I'm Dominican, so I'm Hispanic, too." He laughed and shook his head. "You couldn't even get two people for that; you covered them both with one guy. And you got your one token Asian, too, I see.

"Speaking of 3, she's a cutie and a half, man. Something very hot about a sexy woman in a pint-sized teenager's body. It's hard to catch her away from that fucking big guy, 2, though. He's guarding her like a pit bull with a bone. When I do get her alone she says she likes me, but I don't know if she's just fucking with my head or not. I asked for her number, but…shit, what am I telling you for?" He laughed again. "Sorry about that – don't cut off my money! She didn't give it to me, anyway. After we're done with this, she said. That isn't against the rules, right? After we're out of here and in the real world again, we get our lives back.

"Speaking of which, I wonder how my old man is doing right now. My cousin promised he'd look in on him, but that Ace is such a fuck up. He better check in on him, or when I get out of here he'll be sorry. I know I shouldn't really have left my Dad alone to do this, but shit, I'm not working…I need the money. And to be honest? I needed some time away from my Dad, too. I hate to say it, but I feel like I'm in a jail cell in that apartment. I'm only twenty-five years old…I should be out there living a little more, you know? Not taking care of a grouchy old man like a fucking nurse…"

A babble of excited voices came to 6 from the other side of the confessional's door, and he took this as his cue to bring his daily monologue to an end. And so, curious, he rose from the chair and threw the door open to see what the hullabaloo was about. Across the spacious banquet hall, he noted three people gathered at one of the large windows. He strode toward them, calling ahead in a voice that reverberated off the high ceiling, "What's up?"

Bearded and balding 8 looked over his shoulder and said, "We heard breaking glass outside. I don't know if one of the windows above us just fell out of its frame on its own, or if somebody up there broke it."

Hunched at one of the less foggy panes that made up the composite window, not taking his eyes off the scene outside, 10 said, "I told you guys how 9 and I saw someone running around screaming in that brick building. We've either got a loony homeless person, a teenager fucking with us, or Dr. Onsay trying to freak us out."

Peering through the cloudy glass beside him, 9 protested, "And I told you what I think that was. This place is haunted, and I bet Dr. Onsay knows it, and this is all about how we'll react to it."

"Maybe it was one of our lovesick lovebirds doing a suicidal swan dive," 8 said.

"Who?" 9 asked.

"2 and 3."

"Wait – what's that, in the grass?" 10 exclaimed.

6 drew close to another of the panes, tried cleaning it with the heel of his hand but the view remained blurry. All

he could discern was a dark, uncertain shape moving erratically in the tall yellowed grass and drifts of brown fallen leaves. "Is that a dog?"

"Shit…it's a person, and they're hurt," 8 said. "That glass we heard – I think somebody did jump right through a window up there!"

"Oh my God," 9 gasped.

"How'd they get through the bars that are on the windows?" 10 asked.

"They obviously did somehow."

"I'm not so sure that's a person," 6 said.

8 watched the black, flopping form sink down out of sight within the overgrown weeds. He waited for it to resurface. It did not. The stirring grass had gone still. "If it was a badly injured person," he said, "they either just passed out, or died."

"Well, we can't get outside, apparently," 10 said, "but we'd better go upstairs and see if we can figure out what happened."

9 said, "One of us should stay here and keep an eye on the window."

"Okay, you do that. You others with me?"

"Let's do it," said 6.

"They should really let us have a cell phone for emergencies," 9 said, "they really should."

"I've got an idea," 8 said. "I'll go in the confession room and tell them what we saw. Maybe they'll be listening, and come around to check things out."

"Good idea, man," 10 agreed. "Go for it."

"Okay," 8 said, then turned to jog across the room toward the confessional's door.

10 nodded to 6. "Let's go, then."

*****

"Someone was saying that the freaky graffiti in here was making them dizzy," said 8. He was sitting in the padded office chair, talking to the wall in between biting his nails and spitting little shreds of them onto the floor. "I can't remember who. But I think it's the drugs we take every morning. What are those things doing to us, huh? I mean, why are we even taking them?"

He felt a light tickling sensation on his upper right arm, and thinking it might be a spider, quickly pushed up the short sleeve of his scrub top. There was no spider, only his tattoo which spelled out ONE LIFE. He studied these words oddly, like the proverbial buffoon who is mystified at a tattoo they received while drunk. But as if he finally recognized it, he let his sleeve drop back into place to resume talking. Only, he forgot what it was he had wanted to say.

"Definitely your drugs messing me up," he said accusingly. "I hope I'm not fucking up my health for the rest of my life for a measly four thousand dollars." In truth, since he had been laid off from his job as a mechanical engineer, these days four thousand dollars was far from measly to him. It wasn't bad at all, considering the test's time span. But as 8 considered all this, he realized he couldn't remember how long they had already been there. In fact, he could no longer remember how many days, or weeks, the test was to encompass in total.

Thinking of his former job now, he recalled how his coworkers had dubbed him Scotty, after the character in the TV program *Star Trek*. He chuckled as he related this fact aloud. "Well, you have my name, so you know why they called me that. Sometimes when the floor managers called me to come look at one of the machines in the plant, I'd answer the phone in a Scottish brogue. I'd tell them I'd need two hours to fix something, and they'd play along and say, 'You've got fifteen minutes, Mr. Scott.'" He chuckled some more. "Hey, you know what my favorite Scotty moment was? It was in one of the movies, the one where they went back in time to Earth. They needed some repairs done to the ship, so Scotty gave some technology to the guy who was destined to invent that technology. But since Scotty is the one who *gave* the guy the technology, the guy never had to invent it. So...it's like the technology never got invented, it just – *became!* That's a weird loop, huh? Trippy.

"Ohh...God. Speaking of trippy," he groused, his good humor fading, "I'm feeling sooo...I don't know, right now. You're making me have seconds thoughts about all this, you fuckers." To his own ears his words sounded increasingly groggy, or drunken. He felt like he could fall asleep right here and now...take a nap right in this chair. "You think I haven't been through enough stress already, getting laid off – and my Mom dying of uterine cancer last year? And what I went through as a kid? Did you know my father left us when I was only eight? And that business with good old Father Ryan. He's dead now – may he burn in Hell."

*****

2 and 3 were exploring again, like restless zoo animals pacing in their cage. What else was there for them to do, when they weren't eating or sleeping or washing their clothes or bodies?

Gradually, as they walked along on a second floor level, 3 had turned oddly melancholy and philosophical, and she murmured, "Who knows what they used to do here? People worked here for years, and laughed together, and got excited if their friend was going to get married or have a baby, and they all looked forward to Christmas and vacations. Maybe old people came here to live the end of their lives, and lay here feeling lonely and helpless and neglected. There had to be so many people in these rooms doing this or that or whatever, and now maybe everyone who ever worked or lived here is dead. All gone now."

They continued along until they came to a staircase, and without needing to consult each other ascended it together, though 2 glanced sideways at 3, wary of her sulky mood.

"Wow," he said when they arrived at the top of the stairs, now looking down a broad hallway with large composite windows on either side, its ceiling and walls flaking away and the floor covered in these fallen flakes, like a carpet of autumn leaves. The plaster under the paint was crumbling, and radiators against the walls here and there encrusted with rust. "I feel like I could get lockjaw just breathing the air in here."

In their wandering they had passed into a structure that appeared to be situated halfway between the building that served as their base camp, and the old brick building directly across from it – though it was hard to tell exactly where one of the buildings in this complex ended and another began. Were they discrete buildings, after all, or just wings of a single building, like the limbs of one great body?

At the far end of the corridor was a door painted emerald green. 2 started forward, as if its vivid color mesmerized him. 3 hesitated. "I'm getting tired – maybe we should go back. I think I could use a nap."

"Hold on," 2 said. "Let's just look at what's beyond here, for a minute."

"Why?" she asked, growing irritated, but after it was

apparent he wasn't going to turn back she huffed and started after him.

"I just feel...this door looks familiar."

"Why? How could it be familiar?"

"I didn't say it made any sense."

When they reached the end of the hallway, the door proved to be made of green-painted metal. 2 shoved it inward and it groaned and squealed on its hinges, resisting him. In the end it became stuck about halfway open, but it was enough for 2 to slip into the room beyond. 3 followed.

It was a fair-sized chamber without windows, water-damaged, some of its scaly ceiling fallen away to reveal its slatted understructure, the scabby mottled walls looking diseased. As always, whatever machines had formerly operated here (had the complex been a factory) or beds resided here (had it been a hospital) were gone as if they had never existed. But there was one interesting feature in the room. In one corner, as if cowering together in fear, stood four chairs. With their metal frames and torn vinyl seats showing the spongy padding inside, they were identical to the chairs that stood around the table in the banquet hall. And piled upon this grouping of chairs were four rolled-up sleeping bags. They appeared new, and identical to those in which 2 and 3 and the others slept every night.

"Spares?" 2 wondered aloud. He walked to them, took one sleeping bag down and opened it up, spreading it on the debris-covered floor. "Yeah, definitely, same as ours."

3 approached the quilted sleeping bag, got down on hands and knees upon it and smelled the area in which a person's head would rest. "Huh," she said.

"What?"

"I can smell the soap we all shower with. Someone's been using this. Maybe the testers have been camping in this room all along, and we didn't know it? Or do you think there could even be another group of subjects in this place with us?" 3 felt something under her knee, changed her position and unzipped the bag further. She reached inside, took hold of an object and drew it out to examine. "Ugh!" she exclaimed.

"What's that doing in there?" 2 asked.

She held the small head of a doll with long, bleached-blond hair. 3 flung it away from her, across the room. "Weird," she said with distaste, but she then rolled onto her back and stretched her body out fully. "God I'm so tired. Maybe I should just nap here."

2 stood over her, gazing down. "That sounds like a good idea," he said.

"Why don't you open a bag, too?" she said, holding his gaze. "And we can take a nap together?"

"That sounds like a good idea," he repeated. "Maybe I'll open up all the bags, so we'll have plenty of room to take a nap."

"Sounds like a good idea," she echoed, smiling subtly.

So 2 took down one rolled sleeping bag after another to unfurl them and spread them on the floor together. In so doing, tucked into each of the bags he discovered another disembodied doll's head, each doll different in style. "Why would anybody do that?" he asked.

"Get rid of them," 3 said. "They give me goose bumps." She embraced her own bare arms.

Having tossed the last severed doll's head into a far corner, 2 got down on their thin makeshift mattress and stretched out beside her. "If you're cold," he offered in a soft voice, rubbing at the raised bumps on one of her arms, "maybe I can make you warm."

*****

10 and 6 had mounted a series of cement staircases to a third floor landing. Here they came upon a corridor with its right-hand wall masked by graffiti, its far end lost in gloom. They could see enough, however, to tell that some of the black paint had run down from the wall and puddled on the hallway's floor. What drew their attention, though, was a large window facing onto the stairwell. Bars covered it, but the glass was shattered outward. As the two men approached it, 6 wondered, "Could someone squeeze between the bars?"

"Maybe, but I don't think they could dive through the glass between the bars."

"Maybe they broke it first and then squeezed through."

"Or maybe nobody jumped out at all."

"So what was that we saw in the grass?"

"Whatever it was," 10 stated, gazing through the large gap broken in the pane, "it isn't down there now."

6 grunted in assent. "Yeah. Did they get up and walk away?"

"Like I say, maybe it wasn't even a person."

"Hey…look," 6 said. "There is something."

Now both men noticed that in the spot where they had seemed to observe a figure from the banquet hall's windows, a nest of numerous black filaments floated and rippled in a breeze, which rustled through the tall grass with which the strands blended. As the men watched, one after another of these whipping strands became dislodged and airborne…until within only moments of their first noticing them, all of the thin black streamers were gone.

"What was that?" 10 asked. "Some trash or something somebody threw down there?"

"Guess it was. Guess that's what we saw: trash."

10 then realized that white flecks were also being borne

along in the breeze. "Hey," he asked stupefied, "is that snow?"

"Snow in summer?" 6 said. Then, perplexed, he added, "It *is* summer, isn't it?"

6

9 backed away from the window in the banquet hall, unnerved by what she had witnessed only moments after the men had left the room: the sudden eruption of writhing, swirling black threads and ribbons, like the tendrils of some huge inverted jellyfish, as if a monstrous plant had suddenly bloomed from the place in the overgrown grass and weeds where there had appeared to be a human figure. Then, the rapid dissolution of that weird plant, its streamers swimming away and dispersing on the snow-spitting wind. And now there was nothing, as if she had only imagined it all.

Damn 10 and 6, for having left her alone here. Shouldn't one of them, at least, have offered to go sit in the confessional in case Dr. Onsay or someone else were listening, and let them know there was an emergency? Someone, maybe even one of their team, apparently having fallen or jumped from an upper story? Might there be someone lying there still, and she just couldn't see them for all the ground cover?

She would do it herself, she decided, turning with determination to march across the cavernous room toward the closed confession chamber's door.

9 threw open the door to the closet or former restroom that served as their confessional. Its single padded office chair stood empty, and so she shut the door after her and

moved forward to seat herself.

******

2 dreamed of large snails with spiral shells like rolled-up sleeping bags, and the smiling rubber heads of dolls. These snails traced slow, aimless paths across a floor carpeted with fallen flakes of paint and crumbs of plaster.

He could hear the long clomping strides of a giant – and yet he never saw this giant. The invisible titan's steps would grow thunderously louder as it approached one of the oblivious snails. Then suddenly, the snail would flatten, crushed under the invisible being's foot, the shell shattered like a clay pot. The rubber head would go rolling away, still smiling. And from the broken snail shell would spread a sticky puddle, as black as ink…

2 opened his eyes to hear the ponderous, clomping steps of the giant.

He sat up abruptly, saw that 3 was curled asleep beside him, her small brown body covered by the flap of one of the sleeping bags. Those slow pounding steps were growing louder, louder as they approached down the hallway beyond the metal door. Eyes fixed on that emerald green door, which he had managed to push shut again earlier, he reached over to take hold of 3's leg through the padded sleeping bag and shook her.

"What?" she grumbled, shoving his hand away.

"Get up!" he whispered urgently. "Somebody's coming!"

3 lifted her head, grimacing. Then, as she finally registered the encroaching crashing sound, she scrambled to her feet, gathering up her strewn clothing. 2 was already on his feet doing the same.

2 had just finished lacing his sneakers when the

clomping sound stopped right outside the green metal door. There were several weighted seconds of silence, and then a sound like the dying groan of a sinking ship as its iron hull collapses. Something was shoving at the door.

"Who's there?" 2 demanded. 3 had simply cried out inarticulately, and leaped behind him, holding onto his waist.

Despite its resistance, the door was opening inward in fits and starts. 2 looked around him for a weapon. But why, he asked himself, did he feel he needed a weapon?

The door had shifted enough to admit a large greenish head like that of a giant turtle. But it was soft, boneless, as the probing head squeezed into the room. Not an animal's head, but only a rolled sleeping bag. Following this came a slim, white figure. A woman in white clothing. But she was dragging something behind her that wedged in the narrow space, not soft and pliable like the sleeping bag.

"Jesus!" 3 said, angry for having been so afraid.

2 walked across the room to grab hold of the metal door's latch, and he tugged on it with all the weight of his tall, large body. It squealed open enough for 5 to pull into the room the chair she had been dragging after her. The chair which, as it bounced up the stairs beyond the hallway and across the floor of the hallway itself, had sounded like the thudding stride of a giant.

It was another of the chairs, with metal frame and vinyl padding, in which the test subjects would sit at the banquet hall table.

"What are you doing with these?" 2 asked 5 as he stood before her.

The woman looked up at him blankly. Like a sleepwalker, he thought. Then, in a similarly distant voice, she spoke. "I thought I'd store these things in here."

"Did you put the rest of this stuff in here?" he asked

her.

5 looked past him, at the chairs clustered in the corner and the four sleeping bags overlapping upon the floor. "I don't think so."

"Well why bring this stuff in here now?"

"Well, because we're not using it."

"What do you mean, we're not using it?"

"We don't need it. We have five chairs and five sleeping bags downstairs. That's enough for all of us, isn't it?"

"Enough?" 2 began, exasperated. But then he paused, stared into 5's face for a few moments, and resumed, "Yeah…yeah, that's all we need."

******

That night, with the large windows so black they might have been painted over, and the bloodless glow of fluorescent lights illuminating the banquet hall, the five of them collected the dinners that dropped down the PVC pipe into the plastic bucket and took them to the Formica-topped table to eat. On one side of the table, 3 sat with 2 to her left and 5 to her right. Opposite them sat 6 with 10 on his right.

As she removed the humble dinner fare from a paper bag with her number penciled on it, 5 glanced over at the PVC pipe that speared up through the high ceiling, and said in a low voice, "Someone is definitely in the building with us, upstairs. Next time one of us should sneak up there and look around when we know it's time for them to send down our meal."

"And do what?" 6 asked. "What are they doing wrong by being in the building? They're just conducting the test, right? Why do you need to catch them at it?"

5 looked at him, her expression vague, and said nothing, returning her attention to her meal.

"What's funny," 10 said, flattening his paper lunch bag on the table in front of him and smoothing it out with his hands, "is, why assign us these particular numbers? Why am I 10? What's the significance of 2, 3, 5, 6, and 10?"

"What do you mean?" 3 asked.

"I mean, the implication is that there are gaps. Missing numbers."

Chewing, 2 shrugged and said, "Who knows what their test system is? What does it matter to us?"

10 grunted, but he seemed unsatisfied, his brow rumpled as if in troubled thought. He had the aspect of one trying to recall a disturbing dream that had slipped away upon waking.

"So anyway," 6 said, "I don't know what to make of what 10 and I saw from the window up there. Maybe someone just threw a bag of rubbish out the window or something, and it opened up and all this crap blew away. A person couldn't get between those bars easily…unless it was you." He smiled across at 3. "And we didn't see any body down there."

"Maybe it was part of the test," 2 said, "and they're just fucking with us."

5 turned to stare across the room at the imposing black windows. Reflected in their multiple panes, along with the fluorescent tubes overhead, she saw their gathered reflections. Her own floating face gazing back at her, with eyes lost in black pools of shadow like those of an empty mask. Small and distant, as if it were being sucked away into the night beyond.

"I wonder how much longer we have to go in the test?" she mumbled, more to herself than anyone. "Seth…Seth might be missing me."

The others, not knowing of whom she spoke, did not reply.

"And my Mom," 5 went on in her dreamy voice. "She needs me. She's dying of cancer, uterine cancer, and I watch TV with her in the hospital."

"I take care of my Dad, too," 6 told her. "Don't worry, I'm sure we'll be finished with this soon."

Sipping tap water from his tumbler, 2 eyed 5 surreptitiously over its plastic rim. Earlier, before they had left the room where he and 3 had napped, a thought had occurred to him and he had taken the rolled-up sleeping bag from 5's hand. She hadn't resisted. He had unrolled and unzipped it, and inside uncovered yet another doll head – the fifth doll head to be tossed across the room. When he'd asked 5 if she had hidden the plastic head inside the bag she had professed to know nothing about it, but he was suspicious about this. He was still not satisfied with her answer about storing the sleeping bag and chair in that room because they weren't needed. She had seemed so out of it, and didn't look all that much more with it now. But then, he had to admit he wasn't feeling all that sharp himself. The pills they took every morning…it probably had to do with that. He was beginning to become concerned about them. But how could he avoid taking them, when their ritual was to watch each other do so? Could he hold six pills in his mouth without swallowing them, and when the others were looking away return them to his hand? But what if cameras were indeed watching their every move, and he forfeited his four thousand dollars?

Having finished their meal, they crumpled the paper bags and – per the instructions they had received upon having been accepted as test subjects – dropped them into a hole that had been cut into the floor not far from the plastic bucket in which their bags of food and pills were deposited. Watching his balled-up bag plummet quickly into darkness, 10 speculated that another PVC pipe must be fitted to this hole, to direct all their trash into a bin or such on a basement level below. But why be so fastidious about trash when this entire place was in such a state of ruin? Perhaps it was a condition imposed on the researchers by the owners of this property.

His eyes shifted to the plastic bucket, positioned under the PVC pipe. He remembered at one of their first breakfasts, one of the team moving the bucket aside and peeking up through the thick tube, calling, "Hallooo!" Which one of them had that been, again? He couldn't remember that part.

"Well, I'm going to do my laundry, I guess," 3 sighed.

"I'll go get mine and join you," 2 told her.

"Me, too!" 6 said.

2 turned and looked at him with a faint scowl.

"I think I'm just going to go to bed early," said 5.

"I've still got to do my confession," 10 said. He was about to start across the room toward the confessional when something caught his eye – an object on the floor behind the plastic bucket. As he heard the others dispersing behind him, he squatted down, moved the bucket to one side, and picked up the object he had spied.

It was just another balled-up brown paper lunch bag. But why behind the bucket and not dropped down the trash chute? He vaguely recalled now, maybe at the same breakfast he had just been thinking about, one of their team tossing his bag across the room as if launching a basketball at a hoop, and missing. Who had it been? Again, he couldn't remember that much of it. Idly, not even truly curious, he opened up the wadded paper to view the number that was certain to be penciled on it.

"Huh," he said, perplexed.
The number was 8.

7

"The pills make us forget, don't they?" 10 said. "But I suspect that's the least of what they do.

"There was a woman I was attracted to. 5 and 3 are attractive, but it was someone else, I'm sure of it. Maybe it was even you, Dr. Onsay, since conveniently I can't remember much about you…how to spell your name, what your voice sounded like, or even exactly what you looked like. Huh – one of the others told me they even thought you were a man. I can't remember who it was, now, who said that…

"Or was it subject 8 I was attracted to? You know who I'm talking about, even if I don't. I found a lunch bag with the number 8 written on it, so there was at least one other subject…which means, there may have been others, too. Others to fill in the gaps. 1, 4, 7, 8, 9. Another team of five to our team of five? Were they removed? Or are they still here somewhere? Are we supposed to figure this out as part of the test, or are you trying to hide these things from us? I feel like I knew so much more than I do now.

"It bothers me a lot, forgetting things, I'll tell you straight. You want to know why? Of course you do.

"My wife and I divorced when our son was only two years old. She took him out to California to hook up with some kid she met online playing *World of Warcraft.* And I do mean kid; he's fifteen years younger than her. Can you believe that? Just twenty-five, with a forty year old woman. Horny little fucker. Yeah, she looks okay now, but is he going to stick with her through menopause? I think that will give him pause. Oh, he said he'd take care of her and our son. But guess what? They've been struggling since day one, and even though our divorce was uncontested and I'm not obligated to pay her child support, I still send her two hundred dollars a month. I don't mind caring for my child, believe me – it actually makes me feel better to do it – but it's the point. She believed her pimply Blood Elf would keep her in gold sovereigns.

"But what I'm getting to is, she moved out there two years ago. The baby is four now. When I got my ass downsized at work I was finally free to go out there and visit him, because God knows she can't afford to come out here. Now, when that baby was two I was the sun to him…I was like his God. That *smile* he had for me. Always throwing himself on me, climbing all over me, sitting in my lap while I showed him cute videos on YouTube, bringing his toys to me so we could play together, and crying hysterically if I left the house just to run for cigarettes. See, I never had a kid before. I married late, and became a father late. He was the sun to me, too.

"Well, you know where this is going. When I came in their apartment and he saw me, he ran into the other room and hid behind the sofa. When I bent down and tried to pick him up, he cried. Cried hysterically, the same as when he used to think I was leaving him. He didn't recognize me. No – more than that. He'd forgotten me. Forgotten me totally.

"Can you imagine forgetting the sun? But he did.

"I can't entirely blame her…the bitch. I should never have agreed to let her take him out of state. I should have found time to go visit him sooner, work be damned.

"Well…I haven't visited him since. Maybe someday. Someday we can start again from the beginning…"

10's voice broke, and his words tumbled away into silence. Silence, except for one half-suppressed sob. He leaned back in the office chair with his palms pressed into his eye sockets, struggling for self control. He was feeling queasy. Queasy and oddly, utterly drained.

"I'm tired," he lamented. "Tired of this life. It's only disappointment upon disillusion upon disgust. Pointless strife. What do I have to show for it? What?

"It isn't that I would ever kill myself. But sometimes I just wish a bus or a meteor would hit me. Sometimes I just wish I was never born at all."

Then, 10 heard a muffled commotion out there, somewhere beyond the shut confession chamber's door. He didn't get up to investigate, however. He didn't even have the strength to remove his hands from his eyes. Sleep was the best thing right now. No…forgetting was even better. Forgetting everything. Forgetting himself…

****

"I'm sure it wasn't here before!" 5 exclaimed. "I'm sure of it!"

2 studied the mural of black and white graffiti that plastered one cinderblock wall of the room the women had been using as a dormitory. He had never been in this room before, since the men had their own dormitory in which to tuck themselves in the warm envelopes of their sleeping bags, but 3 confirmed, "She's right. I don't remember this being in here, either."

"So did someone paint all this just in the time we were having our dinner?" 6 asked. "It doesn't even look wet." He reached forward to touch it, but 5 cried out. Startled, he looked at her.

"Don't!" she hissed, wide-eyed.

"They painted this and the other ones, just since the last time we were in these rooms?" 2 said. He was certain the graffiti that now covered one wall of the men's dormitory, which he had discovered when he'd gone to collect his dirty laundry, had not been there previously either. He was *dead* certain. And then there was the mural of graffiti that now obscured one wall in the room where the new washer and dryer had been provided for them. And the murals that concealed one wall in the men's shower room, and one wall in the women's shower room. "Five new murals? And we didn't catch them making these? What happened, did we all fall asleep at the dinner table for a couple of days?"

"How many murals does that make now?" 6 asked.

They tallied them up together, and came to the number nine. The one in the confessional – the only mural that extended beyond a single wall, encompassing as it did all four. The new murals in the male and female sleeping rooms, the male and female showers, and the laundry room. A mural 2 and 3 had stumbled on in a brick hallway. Another 5 had encountered in the basement of the mildewed old building across the way. The mural 2 and 3 had come across on the third story, that had dribbled paint onto the floor and through the ceiling of the level below. And who could say whether there might be more? They all felt that they had only touched the tip of the iceberg in exploring this complex, had only done so idly, without a clear purpose or determined effort to map it all out. For why should they? Still, because of this, the place seemed like an enormous, even infinite maze to them.

"They're part of the test," 2 murmured. "But why? What are they for? What do they do?"

He scrutinized the mural before them more closely. As closely as he could, but its boiling turmoil of shapes seemed to pull his eyes, pull his mind, in all directions at once. He recognized certain designs by now, including the symbol for infinity, but there seemed to be layers or depths that his eyes had not formerly plumbed…patterns that only now made their presence partly known. Background areas of black or white – over which the tagging had been layered – that had previously appeared random to him now looked to be made of interlocking forms, like those of an artwork by Escher: white shapes morphing into white birds, interacting with black shapes morphing into black birds. And the more he stared at this half-hidden map of black continents in oceans of milk (or white continents in oceans of ink?), the more complex the hinted patterns became. Were there even interlocking tesseracts like a multidimensional scaffolding upon which all the rest hung? And then, the tesseracts themselves composed, of course, of all those innumerable 0s and 1s.

5 pivoted around to look through the open doorway of the women's sleep chamber. "Hey, where's Te–" she began.

"Who?" said 6.

She peered through the threshold with a slack mouth for several beats, then shook her head as if to clear it and said, "Nothing."

8

The next morning, at the breakfast table, 2 found it much easier to avoid swallowing his daily ration of pills than he'd thought. When he brought his hand up to his mouth – atypically, as if to swallow all six of the pills in one go – he simply closed his fingers around the variety of gel capsules and tablets. As a bit of sleight of hand, magician's misdirection, he raised his left hand with the tumbler of water at the same time he lowered his right hand with the palmed pills. Under the table, he tucked them into his waistband.

His performance was not noted, in any case. By now the ritual had become so second nature that the other three subjects didn't even glance at him to verify his compliance. He just prayed that no one watching through a hidden camera had detected his trickery.

2 wasn't even entirely sure why he had done it. He was a math teacher, his realm of expertise one of immutable order and hard rules. He would have expected one of the others, maybe young 6, to be more the rebel. Though who was to say 6 had actually taken his own pills just now?

Surely they couldn't be seriously harmful, even if this was a trial for a new series of pharmaceuticals. Why then? Why had he felt he must purge his system of these unknown chemicals?

At the same time, there were other drugs which he still

craved, though he had been denied them since the test had begun. He said aloud, "Man oh man, would I love some coffee right now. And more than that, a cigarette. I swear I could strangle a puppy for a cigarette."

To his immediate left, 3 looked up at him and said, "I didn't know you smoked."

He blinked at her. "Of course. Of course I smoke. I, ah, I just haven't been able to, so that's why you haven't seen me."

"Oh." She shrugged. "Me, too."

"What? Really? Are you kidding now?"

"No. You just haven't seen me because I haven't been able to, either."

"Oh. Wow. Well, you should quit that."

"I will if you do."

"Looks like we're already working on that."

3 looked him up and down, and smiled. "I thought people got fat when they quit smoking. I swear you've been getting thinner. When I first met you, you had more of a gut."

"A gut? Thanks."

"Well, you don't now. You look sexier."

2 chuckled, shy in front of the others but pleased. From the corner of his eye he saw 6 look across the table at them, his tumbler paused on its way to his mouth. 2 wanted to tell 3 she looked as sexy as ever, but decided to save the compliment for when they were alone.

Finished with her meal, 5 got up from the table, stretched with an exaggerated yawn, and wandered across the room to one of the towering windows. She called hollowly across the room to the others, "Wow, it's really snowing out there now. You should see it – everything is white."

While 3 finished her modest meal, 2 and 6 joined 5 at

the window. "Huh, yeah," said 2, observing the blizzard. "It looks like the whole world's being erased."

2 glanced back at the Formica-topped table around which their four chairs were grouped, to see if 3 was finished and ready to have a look outside for herself. He was surprised to see that she was gone from the room instead. The four chairs stood empty.

****

5 left the banquet hall, proclaiming that she would be taking a shower, leaving 2 and 6 alone. 2 didn't want to make conversation with the younger man, so he busied himself with exploring the room's furthest reaches: the far wall opposite that in which the great windows were set. Here, and spaced elsewhere in the enormous room, a cast iron radiator with leafy scroll designs stood against the wall of glazed white bricks. Nearing it, 2 established that it was functioning, giving off heat to keep the wintry weather outside at bay. Not far from the radiator, lying flush with the wall and apparently overlooked by whomever had stripped this complex to the bones, he spotted a few varied lengths of old copper pipe, blotched green with verdigris. He lifted one of these, about three feet long and with a ninety degree elbow at one end. Hefting it in two hands like a baseball bat, he regarded how good it might serve as a weapon.

A weapon? And why was he thinking about that?

Still, he carried it back to the table with him and rested it across the imitation granite surface. He saw that 6 had busied himself with an ersatz game of basketball, repeatedly launching a balled-up paper lunch bag, probably his own, toward the white plastic bucket in which their three daily meals dropped.

Both men looked around as 5 reentered the room, walking briskly and with a fretful expression. When she arrived at the table, 6 drew in closer to hear what she had to report.

Out of breath, 5 whispered, "Just now I accidentally walked in on 3 when she getting ready to take a shower. She hadn't turned the hose on yet, so I didn't hear her in there. I don't think she saw me in the doorway – I was only there for a second."

"And?" 6 asked.

"Anyway, she was naked, and I couldn't believe it but…she has a penis. 3 is really a guy!"

2 hissed, *"What?"*

"I think she hid it from Dr. Onsay. Don't you see how this might throw the test off? There's supposed to be two guys and two girls, right? I'm sure that arrangement was intentional. But now it's really three guys and just one girl – me!"

6 said, "She's not a guy. Impossible."

"I know what I saw!" 5 insisted.

"You said you only saw her a second."

"Look, I'm telling you she has a cock – I saw it plain as day!"

"And I'm telling you she doesn't have a cock," 6 retorted.

"How would you know?"

"Because I've seen her plain as day, too."

2 turned toward 6. "What do you mean, you've seen her plain as day? When did this happen?"

6 looked sorry at what he had blurted. "Yeah, I know…you've seen her, too, haven't you?"

"I asked you when and how did you see her?" 2 growled through gritted teeth.

"Look, before you get all violent, here, it's her you

should be taking this up with if it bothers you, not me."

"But who knows," 5 said as if weighing the matter alone, oblivious to the tension between the two men, "maybe Dr. Onsay is aware of it – maybe 3's discussed it in confession – and it doesn't matter if I'm the only woman, after all."

"Fuck this," 2 snarled. "I'm going to go talk to her right now."

"You're going to walk in the shower and ask her to show you her cock?" 5 said, snapping out of her pensive state.

"She does not have a fucking cock!" 2 shouted. "But apparently she's had this motherfucker's cock."

"Fuck you, man," 6 snapped. "What are you, her husband or something?"

2 began stomping across the room. "Suck my dick," he called back over his shoulder.

"Ah, go suck her dick!" 6 returned.

5 faced 6 with a furrowed brow and said, "I thought you said she didn't have a dick."

Exasperated, 6 told her, "I'm just giving the guy shit, now!"

****

When 2 stepped into the women's shower room, its new mural of graffiti shiny with sprayed water as if its paint was not yet dry, 3 looked up at him with a gasp, pressing a hand flat between her adolescent breasts with their pronounced dark brown nipples. Her hair was plastered to her neck, water beaded on her tiny body with its barely defined hips. Nestled under a wiry black thatch of hair, her penis was shaded a darker brown than the rest of her skin, small and uncircumcised.

"Oh thank God," 3 said, "it's only you."

2 stared at her in horrified awe, wagging his head. "I can't believe this…I can't believe it. It's true!"

"What's true, honey?"

He coughed up a laugh. "Oh, so now I'm honey, huh?" He pointed. "You have a cock…you actually do have a cock! You're a *guy!*"

3's brows lowered, her expression darkening. "What are you saying? You act like you didn't know. You didn't kind of notice this before, when we made love up in that storeroom?"

"But…but I fucked you…"

"Ah, yes. In the ass. Are you saying you don't know the difference? Come on now, are you going crazy or are you just sorry about it now? At the time you didn't seem to mind. Are the drugs getting to you that much that you really forgot?"

Pressing his palms to his temples, 2 stammered, "I…I'm sorry…"

"Sorry what? Sorry you and me made love?"

"I'm sorry I forgot about…this."

"How could you forget?"

"I don't know. But yeah, I guess now it's coming back to me. I'm sorry – I'm so sorry. It must be the drugs, like you say."

3 wrapped a white terrycloth towel around her glistening body, hiding her manhood from him, still looking doubtful. "So what are you thinking now, about me?"

"Well, I'm just thinking…didn't you say you have one child? A daughter?"

"Not a daughter; a son," 3 replied. "I mean, a stepson. I called him my 'sun.' He's four years old. But he doesn't live with me anymore. He lives in California."

"Oh…yeah…right. I think I remember that now. Your ex's son, huh?" Then 2's befuddlement turned to a flushed red anger. "6 told me he's seen you with no clothes, too. So you fucked him, didn't you? Or should I say he fucked you? Or for all I know you fucked each other!"

"Don't talk to me like that," she said sharply. But then, modifying her tone, she said, "Honey, look, I'm sorry…okay, I had sex with him one time. It was before you and I made love. After that I've barely talked to him again. You told me after this was all over you wanted to be with me. Maybe I didn't give you a straight answer before…maybe I had some doubts, if you really could love me or if I'm only a novelty and you'll get tired of that. But if you're really serious about me, then I want to be with you, too. So you have to forgive me about 6, okay? I didn't…I wasn't sure…maybe I was being greedy. Just try to forgive me and get past it, all right? Please?"

2 moved toward her, and 3 opened her arms to accept his embrace. He crushed her against his much larger body, and nuzzled his nose in her wet scalp. "Forgive me," he said softly, "and I'll forgive you, too. But you're mine now; don't forget."

"I won't," she said huskily, her face against his chest. And below, her penis was becoming erect as it pressed against his body, as well.

Had to be the pills, 2 thought. He was so glad he hadn't taken them this morning. He swore to himself that for however much longer this test endured, he would not take a single one of them again.

9

Exasperated, 5 had to wait for 2 and 3 to vacate the women's shower room before she could finally take her own shower. She didn't want to speculate on the reason for their long delay in emerging. When they did, they both apologized sheepishly as they slipped past her. She wanted to ask 3 if she – he? – intended to continue using this shower instead of the one reserved for the men, but didn't. She supposed it didn't really matter. But again, she fretted that 3's condition might contaminate the research project's aims, if her ambiguous state were not already known. If it did invalidate the test, she damned well better still receive the money that had been promised her.

She stripped, wetted her hair and body with the hand shower, then shut it off to lather herself with soap. Having done that, she activated the spray again and ran it over her head and body to rinse the soap away.

As she was spraying her hair, head tilted forward a bit and the water streaming past her eyes, a presence attracted her attention and she shifted her gaze to the new wall of graffiti. A person appeared to be standing in front of the wall with their arms hanging at their sides, watching as she showered, and yet the figure was unnaturally dark as if silhouetted. Startled, 5 raised her head and soapy water promptly ran into her eyes. She sputtered, stumbled back, rubbed her free hand over her face. Finally her burning eyes cleared, but when they did she saw no shape standing in front of the mural. Whipping around, she saw no one anywhere within the small room with her. Had there been, but they'd fled? Or had it only been a trick of the blurring, rippling water across her vision?

A wave of tingling radiated across her neck and back, and gooseflesh swept down her arms. She quickly rinsed off the rest of her body – but didn't spray her head any further, lest she again compromise her vision and make herself vulnerable to another person…or to her own imagination.

****

"Are you familiar with the concept of entropy?" 2 asked. Of course, there was no reply from the four walls that boxed him in the confessional. He had told 3 he needed to make his daily Reconciliation before he retired for the night. Not being a Catholic, she hadn't recognized the term for confession until he'd explained it to her.

"Entropy is more in the realm of physics than mathematics, but I always had greater aims than just being a math teacher. I wanted to be a great researcher, a pioneer, a mad fucking scientist…an Einstein or Hawkins. A Carl Sagan or Michio Kaku would do. But one's dreams break down, don't they, because that's entropy for you.

"Entropy is a measure of disorder, and entropy follows what you call an 'arrow of time,' which means like time it can only go one way – toward greater entropy. The infamous second law of thermodynamics states that the entropy of a closed system will never decrease, but will increase whenever possible. A macrostate is made up of microstates, and it's vastly more likely for a macrostate to contain a greater than lesser number of microstates. That's why it's so much more likely you'll have a bad hand in poker than a straight flush. Like I say, entropy leads inevitably to increased entropy. And so one's ambitions, one's hopes and aspirations, tend to have this way of breaking down into smaller and smaller pieces until they become irretrievable. So compromised they're unrecognizable.

"So I may never become a great scientist. I may have to be content holding onto my chiseled down little math teacher pebble for dear life. But I pray to the God beyond all physics that I can hold onto what's left of the dreams I had for me and 3. I can't tell her, can I, that when I found out the truth about her it was a major blow." He laughed out loud. "Ah…let's not talk about major blow right now. The thing is, I was both kind of dismayed and excited at the same time. On a purely sexual level. On a freaky wild, I've-never-visited-this-exotic-country-before level. But in terms of forming a relationship with this wom…this person. In terms of *marrying* this person, and introducing her to my son and my family and the world as my wife…my feelings are more conflicted than I've let on. I still want to be with her. I still hope we can build something. But…but…" He broke off and sighed, words failing him as he had passed from the halls of science to the jungles of emotion.

"The thing is," he mumbled, in a faraway voice, "I can't remember if I discovered the truth about her up in that storage room on the third floor, or just a short time ago in the mess hall." He shook his head like a dog casting off water. "But what am I saying…of course I discovered it in the storage room. How could we have made love without me noticing a little something like that?" Again he was reminded of the drugs they'd all been taking. Again, reminded of his resolve to no longer take them.

"There's negative entropy, called negentropy, but that's not a reversal of entropy – it's just a measure of organization, sort of the complement to entropy. But can you imagine if we could manipulate that 'arrow of time'…if entropy could be reversed, toward greater and greater order and unity? If we could control that – control time, control physics – then we'd be God ourselves." His voice was growing faraway again, sluggish as his eyelids grew weighted. "We could become whatever we wanted to be, and fulfill all our dreams and potential. We could become the whole that we never otherwise seem able to attain…"

****

6 didn't look forward to sharing the men's dormitory with 2 tonight, after their heated exchange, but he didn't fancy the alternative of dragging his sleeping bag elsewhere to set up camp. The series of rooms they had been using for dorms, showers, toilets, and the laundry were all close in vicinity to the banquet hall, and all had been swept clean before their arrival. Most of the other rooms in this complex appeared to have dusty, chalky, debris-pebbled floors. And truth be told, he found the place eerie, and the proximity of the other test subjects – yes, even including 2 – to be comforting.

But as he turned in early for the night and slipped into his sleeping bag wearing just his boxer shorts, he hoped he fell asleep before 2 came in to join him. He wasn't normally one to back down, but getting into a fight wasn't worth losing four thousand dollars.

The room was warm, its sole radiator giving off heat, and the material of the greenish sleeping bag was thick but light. He thought he'd be successful in cozily drifting off before 2 showed up. He lay on his back, contemplating the tiles in the ceiling. Some of them were missing, leaving empty black gaps. For all he could tell, that was the night sky behind them – or the infinity of space.

Already growing drowsy, he felt that he could hear the faint sifting/hissing sound of falling snow against the building's roof and windows. But that was impossible in here, he knew. Still, it was a soothing kind of white noise, perhaps created by his own mind to accompany him to sleep.

Slumber was about to take hold, but 6 never did sleep on his back, so he rolled onto his left side. In so doing, he saw the figure step out of the graffiti.

It was in the shape of a man, but without clothes, without features, entirely obsidian as if the person had been dipped in glistening black oil. Elastic black strands connected the back of the figure, from head to feet, to the painted wall. It took one slow step forward, and some of the strands stretched thinner and disconnected. The faceless black face turned in 6's direction.

He screamed, screamed shrilly, and thrashed madly to kick himself out of his sleeping bag, which suddenly seemed like more of a straitjacket. The eyeless figure took another slow-motion step across the room toward him.

6 managed to get free, scrambling to his feet. The wet-looking walking silhouette had taken a third step, and the last of the stringy tar tethering it to the wall had snapped, when 6 bolted from the room still shrieking.

****

3 and 5 met him in the hallway. He crashed into them, nearly bowling them both over, and as they held onto 6 to both calm him down and hold themselves up, he looked back over his shoulder with wild eyes.

"What is it?" 5 asked, unconsciously digging her nails into his arms.

"Someone in my room!" 6 panted. "Someone walked out of the wall!"

"*What?*" said 3.

6 babbled in Spanish – "*Fantasma!*" – but then swallowed and tried again. "A ghost! A fucking ghost – in there!" He pointed toward the open doorway to the men's sleeping room.

"Come on," said 3, breaking away from them and striding toward the room purposefully.

6 cried, "Don't!"

"Wait!" 5 called. Though terrified, she started after 3.

If there truly had been an apparition, it would be gone when she looked, 3 thought. Wasn't that the teasing and fickle way ghosts operated? And yet she still had to see for herself…

It was still there.

There was no longer an upright, human-shaped figure stepping across the room. Instead, what 3 and – close on her heels – 5 encountered was a barely anthropomorphic form lying on the floor. This mostly shapeless mass at best resembled a human being bound tightly in a black plastic garbage sack, and as if imprisoned thus and running out of air, the cocoon-like form was squirming and thrashing on the floor in a frenzy. When 6, having mustered his courage, came up behind the two women, he was oddly reminded of himself when he had been struggling to free himself of his sleeping bag.

The flopping black shape on the floor did not utter a sound, but one could discern a shallow concavity that appeared like a rudimentary mouth. A mouth that stretched as if to howl, but couldn't.

5 was screaming, and backed up hard into 6's chest. 3

yelled, "Go get 2!"

"Who?" 6 said, unable to take his bulging eyes off the creature.

3 looked at 6, and a vague desperation seized her. She pushed her way between 5 and 6 and went dashing off down the hallway, in the direction of the confessional. Hadn't 2 told her he would be performing his "Reconciliation"?

****

"Entropy," 2 muttered, like a dreamer. His eyes were slitted half closed. He was a macrostate, being pulled apart into so many microstates. Or was it, somehow, something like the opposite?

3 threw the door to the confessional open, and screeched in terror.

2 was draped heavily in the office chair, his head lolling to one side, slack-mouthed. From all four walls, four walls completely coated in the black and white graffiti, gooey threads extended to 2's body, attached to him like attenuated suckling leeches. Drooping cables like jungle vines that had grown out of the walls to make a nexus of him. He was the center of a black web, a net that had an oddly geometric look to it, as if the angle of each strand were significant. Some of the thicker of these tendrils pulsed like organic things.

"Come on!" 3 wailed, near hysterical. "Wake up! Wake up!" Despite her horror and her aversion to letting any of those creepers make contact with her, she stepped into the room, protected by the outline of the door's threshold where it formed a gap in the graffiti. Hunching low to protect her head as she moved in further, she seized 2 by the ankles. After swiveling him around in the chair to face her, she pulled hard, teeth gritted. 2 slumped down lower in his seat. Gathering her strength, adrenaline flushing through her, she yanked at 2 again. This time he slid out of the chair and onto the floor with a thump. She heard him moan and his head rolled to one side. Many of the connecting strands had snapped free, and their ends wavered in the air like the severed tentacles of an enraged giant squid. 3 started backing toward the doorway, dragging the math teacher's large body across the floor. Fortunately it wasn't far to the hallway, and in seconds he was fully out the door. The last sticky strings broke free of him.

3 reached in to close the door. While countless tendrils still coiled and wriggled in the air, others were receding into the walls and vanishing. 3 slammed the door shut and turned back to 2, knelt down by his side. For a moment she was afraid to touch him, lest whatever had reduced him to this state should afflict her through contact, but then she grasped and shook him. Tears in her eyes, she again shouted, "Wake up! Wake up!" She would have called his name if she'd known it.

2 lifted his head from the floor and blinked at her groggily. "Oh Christ, my back. I think I fell out of my chair and hit my head."

Convulsing with sobs of exhaustion and relief, 3 fell across his body. Confused, though not unappreciative of her concern and the physical contact, 2 slid his arms around her.

****

When from the tail of his eye 6 saw two figures moving down the hallway toward him, he whipped around with a gasp, but was relieved to recognize them as 2 and 3. 3 was holding onto 2's arm, the latter shuffling like an old man and looking pale, sweat filmed on his face. "You got to see this thing, quick!" 6 called. "Before it's totally gone!"

Mesmerized, one hand clamped over her mouth as if she might scream again or even be sick, 5 moved out of the way so 2 could step into the doorway to the men's dormitory and view what lay inside. 3 leaned around his body for a look, as well.

Where before there had at least been a vague semblance of a body, now there was only a gelatinous black heap on the floor. It quivered, pulsated, and it was coming unraveled, ribbons rising up in greater and greater numbers and rippling as if a strong fan were blowing them from below. One by one they came loose from the mass, and almost instantly as they went airborne they dissolved and were gone. With each ribbon torn loose, the mass on the floor diminished that much more.

"It's like the thing we saw outside in the grass," 6 exclaimed. "The same thing!"

"What the fuck is it, though?" 5 said behind her palm. "Ectoplasm?"

"It's like the stuff that was all over 2 just now, in the confessional," 3 told them.

The last bands of black tissue drooped and went limp on the floor, as if all the mass's energy had been spent. Worm-like, these strands writhed across each other but more and more sluggishly. Then, one after another, they grew still and rapidly melted away. Within several more seconds, there was nothing left – not even a stain.

"Was that a ghost?" 6 cried. "I never heard of a ghost like that! What the fuck was it?"

5 looked across the room at the mural of graffiti. "Whoever or whatever it was," she said in a stunned, drugged voice, "they're gone now."

****

2 shoved open the green metal door at the end of the hallway on the third floor. He led the other three subjects into the room in which he and 3 had chanced upon the chairs and sleeping bags grouped in the corner. The bags were still unrolled on the floor where he and 3 had spread them out and made love on them. In a far corner were scattered five doll heads of various sizes, styles and materials.

But in the middle of the room stood a lone, sixth chair with one rolled-up sleeping bag resting on it. The rolled bag made him think of his dream of the giant snails. He was confused; why hadn't he and 3 opened this bag, too? Was this the bag they had seen 5 drag into the room? No…no, he recalled opening that one, finding another doll head. He walked to the chair, took down the new sleeping bag and unfurled it. Sure enough, a sixth doll head was secreted within. He added it to the discarded collection, moved the chair to join the others and lay out the bag on the floor with the rest.

"This is where we're going to sleep tonight," he announced.

"Why?" asked 5.

"Why?" 6 exclaimed. "It's obvious – there's no graffiti in here!"

"We were designated our rooms to sleep in," 5 protested. "Maybe we'll be going against orders if we sleep in here instead, and forfeit everything."

"Why should they have a problem with that?"

"The graffiti showed up in our bedrooms for a reason. They want us to sleep near the graffiti."

"Fuck that," 6 spat. "I'm not sleeping in a room where ghosts walk out of the walls!"

"I'm not sure that was a ghost," 5 said. "Strictly speaking."

"Then what was it?" 6 argued. "If it wasn't a ghost, then that's even worse."

"If I hadn't come in when I did," 3 said, "who knows what would have happened to 2." She looked up at him. "How do you feel?"

"I feel pretty fucking unnerved, is how I feel, after hearing what was happening to me."

"But did it hurt you in any way?" 5 asked.

"I feel confused, and like I could jump right out of my skin."

"But that's just nerves, right? It didn't actually do anything to you."

"That's because I stopped it before it could!" 3 persisted. "If you want to sleep alone beside the graffiti, go ahead; the rest of us want to sleep in here. We should barricade the door with the chairs or something."

"Good idea," said 6.

5 laughed, wagging her head. "Listen to you guys! Yes, some very bizarre things are going on. But it's obviously part of the test we're getting paid to participate in! We signed contracts!"

"They never told us about this crap," 6 said.

"Obviously they didn't tell us for a reason, so as not to contaminate the experiment or something."

"That artwork isn't graffiti," 2 said, pacing the room as if it were a prison cell. "Either it's disguised to look like graffiti, or we've just misinterpreted it as graffiti. It's something else."

"Like what?" 3 asked him.

"It's like a portal, or something. I've looked at it up close. It's all made up of tiny numbers; zeroes and ones. Binary numbers. I don't know why, but it's something weird. It isn't the work of kids with spray cans."

"Okay, what if you're right?" 5 said. "All the more reason not to avoid it. It's obviously something we're meant to interact with. Look, it's in the confessional, the bedrooms, the showers, the laundry…all the places where we live aside from the mess hall. What does that tell you? They do not want us to avoid those rooms!"

"I don't care," 3 said. "I hate to lose the money, but after what I saw in the confessional I won't sleep beside that stuff again. I swear it was trying to suck the life out of 2."

"Oh man, you don't know that," 5 said. "Look, I'm as creeped out as the rest of you, for sure.; I saw that thing, too. And I told you what I thought I saw in the shower with me – probably the same entity. I don't know what's going on, either. But we really have to think about what we're doing, here."

"The place is haunted," 6 stated simply, "and they know it."

"Well, if that's true, maybe they want us to communicate with these spirits or whatever they are, and the graffiti is kind of like a…Ouija board or something that lets them come through. Isn't it kind of exciting besides being scary?"

"Fuck that. Enough. I'm sleeping here – final."

3 looked 2 up and down closely, as if examining him for lamprey-like scars left on his skin where the inky cords had been attached. She didn't detect any discernible marks. Regardless of this, she stated, "I'm not doing any more confessions, either."

"Me neither!" 6 said.

"You will forfeit this test, I swear," 5 said, her tone becoming more sharp.

"I don't care!" 3 snapped.

"We've all done plenty of confessions by now, and we're all okay."

"Well I guess it doesn't happen to us every time we're in there – maybe it's just because 2 fell asleep – or maybe it does happen to us every time but we're kind of hypnotized, and we don't realize it. Maybe we can't see it happening to ourselves, but other people can see it. We don't know because no one has watched anyone else do a confession before."

"Well," 5 retorted, "we're just taking your word for this, really. You're the only one who claims they saw these goopy strings connected to 2."

"Oh, you bitch," 3 hissed. "Are you calling me a liar? Why would I lie about that? We've all seen enough weird things now…we know it's all true, even if we don't understand it!"

2 narrowed his eyes at 5 with fresh appraisal. Since he'd seen her dragging the chair and sleeping bag into this room her behavior had struck him as erratic. He didn't doubt now that she had put the doll heads in the bags; after all, hadn't she been the one who originally discovered them? He said to her, "I don't get you. You were as spooked as anyone by what we saw in that room. But now suddenly you get all calm and adventurous."

"I didn't say I wasn't spooked," 5 insisted. "But yeah, maybe now that we're seeing more clearly what we're here for, what we're *meant* to experience, I'm just accepting it and rising to the challenge like the rest of you should be doing. Per your agreement!"

"Put your money where you mouth is," 3 said, "and go sleep in the girls' bedroom alone tonight, and the rest of us will stay here."

5 stared hotly into 3's eyes for several long seconds, and then said, "Okay. Okay, I will."

"No," 6 said. "Don't do it."

"Go ahead," 3 said. She raised her arms dramatically. "*Rise* to the challenge."

"I will, ladyboy. And I'll collect my four thousand dollars while the rest of you walk out of here with empty pockets. You'll have gone through all of this for nothing."

"Don't go," 2 said. "We don't want you to do that."

"Oh let the bitch go," 3 said, pulling 2 back a few steps by his arm. "Let her be a hero and show off for Dr. Onsay."

5 turned toward the green metal door, which thus far still stood open. She paused in its threshold, and glared back at the other three subjects. "You're going to ruin this whole test."

"So be it," 6 said. "Goodnight, then."

"You'll be sorry."

"I think it's you who'll be sorry, when you wake up with a ghost standing over you," 3 said.

"Well, magic portals or not, I guess we can't run away from ghosts anyway," 5 said, just before she backed into the hallway. "There's one inside every one of us."

10

2 woke with a single blurted sob, and sat up in his sleeping bag. 3 sat up quickly beside him, immediately rubbing his back. "What's wrong, honey? Honey, calm down."

6 sat up, too, eyes unnaturally wide. "What? What is it? What?" He looked around frantically at the room's four walls, as if expecting to see a half dozen faceless figures stepping out of them all at once. From across the room, six scattered doll heads leered at him instead.

2 took several deep breaths, and got out, "I was dreaming about my Mom. God, I wish this test was over with already. How much longer do we have to stay here? When will they let us know?"

Still rubbing his back, 3 asked, "What's wrong with your Mom, honey?"

"She has cancer. Uterine cancer. I hope she's been doing okay without me."

"Ohh…poor honey. Poor Mom. Wow, so many people get cancer, huh?"

"Fuck, man, you gave me a heart attack." 6 drew himself out of his sleeping bag, paced and stretched at the same time. "Hey, I wonder how 5 made out last night. I can't believe she really had the guts to sleep alone down there."

"Well, she did explore that old brick building over

there alone the first time," 2 reminded them. "She's tougher than we gave her credit for."

"We should go down and look in on her."

"Go ahead," 3 said, "I could care less."

"Hey," 2 scolded her, but he was smiling. 3 noticed the tears still in his eyes and wiped them away with her thumbs.

"I think I'm going to be sick," 6 muttered, watching them.

2 glowered at him. "What's wrong?"

"I'm going to go look in on 5. You two lovebirds can stay here and do whatever."

"Maybe we will do whatever," 3 said defiantly.

"Hey, while you're down there," 2 said, "see if our breakfasts have arrived."

"What, you want room service delivered to you?"

"Okay, so don't bring us our food if you don't want to. We'll be down when we're ready. I'll tell you one thing, and I don't care if they're listening anymore: I stopped taking those meds. I suggest you two do the same." "Good idea," 3 said. "This is all too much now."

"Well, wait a second there," 6 said, "that might be going too far. Not sleeping beside the graffiti is one thing, but I'm sure those meds have a lot to do with this whole test, somehow."

"I'm sure they do – but I'm not taking them."

"Whatever, man," 6 said, leaning his back against a wall as he pulled on and laced first one sneaker, then the other. "But I'm not going to stop. I do still want that four thousand bucks, you know."

They watched him haul on the metal door and exit the room, leaving it jammed halfway open behind him. As soon as he had left, 3 turned impulsively toward 2, took his face in her hands and kissed him on the mouth lingeringly. Their tongues swished wetly around each other.

Immediately 2 felt his penis stiffening, at the same time that a drowning klaxon in his mind tried to blare: *I'm kissing a man. Kissing a man…*

But when 3 pulled away from him to regard him with shining eyes, 2 grinned back at her, his nightmare having dissipated. "Thanks for rescuing me last night, sweetie," he said. Then he shrugged. "Apparently, rescuing me."

"I'm not letting them take you away from me," 3 told him firmly. "You and me are sticking together, right?"

He pulled her against him again, his arousal returning as he ran his hand up and down her back. He wondered if they could get away with some quick lovemaking before 6 returned. His hand slipped under the top of her white hospital scrubs, to rub the smooth bare plain of her lower back, as if he were trying to gently wipe away the Mobius strip tattooed there.

Looking over her shoulder at her exposed back, and the blue ink punched into the taut brown skin under his palm, 2 frowned and drew back from her, shifted his body behind hers to pull apart the hem of her top and the waistband of her pants. A tattooed caption under the figure 8 Mobius strip, in flowery script, read: LIFE'S NO STORYBOOK. It wasn't the meaning of the words that confounded him, but he simply couldn't recall having noticed this part of the tattoo when they had made love in this room. Come to think of it, he couldn't recall her body bearing any tattoos at all. Had the rest of her body so distracted him? He decided to make a joke of it while calling the tattoo to her attention. "Nothing personal, honey, but aren't you a little old for this silly tattoo? I mean, you're still as cute as a button, but you being a mom and all…"

3 twisted around and slapped his arm. "You think I'm so ancient? I'm only twenty-eight years old, you know!"

"Twenty-eight," he echoed.

"Yes! I told you that." She cocked her head at him. "Honey, are you okay? You know I don't have any kids, either."

"No daughter…no stepson…"

"No! No nothing! Of course not!" 3 gave him an exaggerated pout of feigned hurt and jealousy. "I think you must be thinking of someone else."

****

5 had awakened early, opening her eyes to find herself confronting the graffiti wall as if she had been staring at it through her closed lids while she had been sleeping. Viewed sideways like this, some of its designs seemed to take on more meaning for her, if only in a subliminal manner, and yet still remained just a notch away from locking into conscious interpretation. She sat up, stretched, emerged from her warm chrysalis.

While showering she watched the graffiti-covered wall avidly, but with more curiosity than nervousness this time. Nothing out of the ordinary occurred, and she dressed and moved out into the banquet hall. Its commanding windows were apportioned into blank white squares. She found four envelopes containing their pills in the bucket, buried under four paper lunch sacks of breakfast. After filling her plastic tumbler with water, she seated herself alone at the table, swallowed each of her pills, then started on her breakfast of apple, banana, and cereal bar with raspberry filling.

She glared at 6's empty chair directly facing her, conscious of 2 and 3's empty chairs to her left. She couldn't believe they were willing to sacrifice that money. Sacrifice *everything.* They were putting her own involvement and investment in this research at risk. Their changed attitude only made her all the more resolved to her own commitment.

As she chewed a crisp mouthful of apple, she allowed her gaze to slide aimlessly along the surface of the table toward its far end. There, someone had set down a length of old copper pipe, blotched green with verdigris, about three feet long and with a ninety degree elbow at one end.

And folded on the table about halfway between the pipe and herself, 5 noted a pair of eyeglasses that someone had also left behind. Curious, she rose from her chair and picked them up, unfolded them. They had narrow lenses set in modern-looking white frames with the name of the designer, Roberto Cavalli, printed on the inside of one arm.

5 contemplated the eyeglasses for several protracted seconds in which she did not move, nor even blink. At length, she said aloud, "I was wondering where these went to." And then she raised the eyeglasses to her face and slipped them on.

When her meal was finished, 5 drifted back to the female dormitory, standing framed in the threshold and gazing upon the black and white graffiti. Right away she grinned, and her heart tripped into a faster rhythm. Right away everything seemed to come together for her at last, like a film of a jigsaw puzzle exploding into thousands of pieces, but played in reverse. It was the lenses of her eyeglasses, she was convinced, restoring her sight after it had been compromised up until now.

Rapturously, she crossed the room, raising both arms as she did so. When she was close enough she lay her hands flat upon the glossily-painted surface of the wall.

A subtle but steady vibration – or was that an electrical current? – trembled up both her arms. Coursed through her veins, shepherding her corpuscles along, and humming along her nerves, plucking at them like the strings of a harp.

She was wet between the legs. Her grin was so broad it hurt her bunched cheeks. Tears of joy ran freely from her eyes, and she moved in closer, hugged the wall as if crucified to it, arms spread wide, chest and the side of her face pressed hard against it.

There was a sense of communion. Communion with an *otherness*, but through that somehow a communion with herself. Like a lover, her quivering lips almost brushing the wall as she spoke, she whispered, "You needed that I worked for a pharmaceutical company. That was one of the things you needed from me. You must have needed things from all of us, to *become*..." Oh, to be *needed*, to be essential even in part. Seth had never really needed her...she saw that now.

She felt as if, for the first time in her life, she had truly come home. Truly found herself. She had never known until now how much her life had always been one gaping wound, as if from birth she had been a walking autopsied corpse with its chest spread wide and red and nearly empty. But now, she was only a few steps away from becoming fully healed, at last.

****

6 had lost interest in 3, no longer felt competitive with 2; the big guy was welcome to her. 6 couldn't reconcile what 5 had said she'd seen in the shower with what he himself had seen when he and 3 had been alone together that one time, and so it was less of a headache (and his head *did* ache when he tried to sort it out) to just drop the whole matter. He had a young girlfriend, Ana, a Dominican like himself and just as diminutive and cute as 3, waiting for him on the outside anyway.

Remembering Ana now made him also recall Dr. Onsay, whose dark complexion had caused him to wonder about the researcher's nationality. Maybe not fully Dominican; a mix perhaps. But there had been the barest tease of accent, and only 6 – when the doctor had introduced himself and given his name – had guessed correctly that name's proper spelling. Spanish being his native language, 6 had known immediately that the doctor's name should be spelled *Once*.

6 had now wandered downstairs to the former base camp, and leaned his head into the female dormitory. "Hello? Hey." No answer, so he stepped all the way inside to find two empty sleeping bags: 5's, and the one 3 had forsaken last night. After a suspicious glance at the wall mural, he went on to look in the laundry area, then stood outside both the female shower room and the female restroom, again calling out for 5. Still no answer. He continued on to the banquet hall.

No sign of her here, the Formica-topped table and its four chairs empty. In the plastic bucket, though, he did find three envelopes of meds and three packed breakfasts. So 5 had already retrieved hers, then. He contemplated bringing 2 and 3 their breakfasts, but decided not to interrupt their probable pre-breakfast feasting, so he simply transferred his own rations to the table. Filling a tumbler at the sink, he debated whether to skip the drugs as 2 had suggested. No…no…he was sure they were too critical to the research; he couldn't risk it.

When he turned away from the sink to approach the table, 5 was standing there directly in front of him and swinging the copper pipe, gripped in two fists like a bat. He dropped his tumbler and the rust-tainted water splashed on his sneakers. The ninety degree elbow at the end of the pipe gashed a dent into 6's forehead above his right eyebrow, blood rising rich and dark in the crater and overflowing it. His eyes had gone wide and he staggered back against the edge of the sink, but he didn't go down, so 5 cocked the pipe back and swung it again. His hands came up too late to intercept it and the elbow struck his nose with a crunch. He dropped to his knees, more blood running from his nostrils and his eyelids fluttering. But he was still upright on his knees. As big as he was, 5 was afraid he would rise up yet and return the attack, so she stepped around behind him and bashed him a third time, now on the back of his head with its close-cropped curly black hair. This time 6 pitched forward onto his face, and when his already shattered nose impacted with the floor it spurted out a thick gout of blood. The gout quickly became a radiating puddle, in which 5 saw her dark reflection.

"You don't want to confess, huh?" 5 said, huffing as she stood over him. Like some torturing inquisitor, through gritted teeth she went on, "I'll *make* you confess."

****

3 had pulled her top off, then taken 2's head in her hands again and drawn it to her chest. He had sucked one of her nipples, dark as a chocolate kiss, into his mouth. His hands were on her waist, but she took one of them off and pressed it to her crotch. "Don't be afraid," she cooed.

From somewhere below came a high-pitched, banshee-like shriek. It reverberated in eerie diminishing waves.

"Jesus!" 2 said, whipping around.

"Was that 5?" 3 said, clutching his arm.

2 jumped to his feet, and waited while 3 hurried her top back on. "Come on!" he said, and they lunged toward the partly open green metal door.

****

5 had had a devil of a time dragging 6 into the confessional, an even harder time pulling his limp body up into the office chair. Once the chair had rolled out from under him and he'd thudded to the floor with 5 sprawled comically atop him. By the time she had succeeded in hoisting him into the chair, her white scrubs were smeared with his blood, making her look like a wartime surgeon. Thank God 6 was still alive. For a while there he had been making an uncanny, bubbly snoring sound, but now a vestige of consciousness had returned and his eyes opened halfway in the mask of thickening blood he wore. He began mumbling. Good. That was very good. "Keep talking," 5 encouraged him as she backed out of the little room, grinning that grin that hurt her face. "Keep talking."

She closed the confessional door, turned and confronted the swath of blood on the floor that led back to the banquet hall. There was no way she could clean that in time; 2 and 3 might come downstairs at any second, and follow the blood here. Disrupt the research more than they already had.

She had retrieved her copper pipe, and held it ready with determination. Maybe she couldn't face both of them at once, subdue them and force them into the confessional as she had 6, but she had done the best she could. The rest she would have to trust to Dr. Onsay. She hoped the doctor would be appreciative of her contribution to the body of work. Now, all that remained was for her to perform one last confession herself. She only had to wait her turn, and pray that she wasn't interrupted before she too could be submerged in the baptismal pool – that she might be reborn.

****

There had been several more unearthly screams, which seemed to penetrate into every room in the entire vast facility. Having thundered down the flights of steps to the ground floor, 2 and 3 followed the last echoing wail to the hallway off which were the entries for the laundry, the restrooms, the shower rooms, and the dormitories. They were advancing down this corridor to begin looking into each room when a figure burst out of the male dormitory.

It charged right at them, letting out an abysmal howl.

****

5 had heard the piercing cries, too, but would not leave her post in front of the confessional to investigate. Anyway, she intuitively understood the source of the screams. They originated from an ephemeral *byproduct*. And didn't that indicate that the process on the other side of the door was complete?

She spun around and swung the door to the confession room open. Yes, it was as she had thought...and she stepped into the room to seat herself in the vacant chair.

****

2 grabbed 3's arm and pulled her against the wall with him just as the running figure plunged past them. In the second that it was beside them, they saw that it possessed a mouth stretched wide but no eyes. It was without hair or clothing as well, completely oily black, and it flashed by them as if unaware of their existence or as if it didn't care about them, so gripped was the entity in the pain or panic that had inspired it to shriek and flee. They turned to watch

the figure, that three-dimensional shadow, continue its charge down the hallway – and yet it had only gone a few yards more before it exploded.

Instantaneously, with a soundless detonation that sprayed like liquid fireworks, the anthropomorphic figure had been reduced to gummy strings and garlands of membrane. The now amorphous mass splatted to the hallway's floor, tendrils of varying thickness flicking madly in the air, in a repeat of what they had witnessed before in the female dormitory.

"God!" 2 choked, crushing 3 against his chest.

Once again, gradually the whipping tendrils broke off, rippled briefly in the air like eels, and dissolved as if they'd lost their transitory hold on corporeality. Once again, the mass was reduced more and more until it utterly vanished, leaving not a trace.

2 released 3, and as they faced each other he said with urgency, "We'd better find 5 and 6."

"What?" 3 said, still looking stunned.

"The others – 5 and 6 – let's find them!" He nodded toward the doorways further along the hallway.

Now 3's expression was one of confusion. "Others?"

2 gaped at her for a second. "The other two…5 and 6. You do remember them, don't you?"

"What are you talking about? There's only you and me in this place."

He took her by the shoulders. "3…listen to me. There are *four* of us! There are two others, a man and a woman. 5 and 6!"

"Honey…" she began, wagging her head.

2 dodged around her then, and took off running down the hallway in the opposite direction from that in which the shadow being had bolted. The drugs, he thought – this was the second morning in which he hadn't taken them, but 3

had only gone without this morning. The drugs were helping her forget…to resort her memories, to readjust, reboot…

"Hey!" she cried, starting after him, "where are you going? Don't leave me here alone!"

2 darted from doorway to doorway, but he met no one in any of the rooms of their base camp: the two dormitories, the showers, the restrooms, the laundry. He moved on, then, toward the banquet hall with 3 on his heels, shouting, "Why are you acting so crazy? Stop it!"

But when he came to a halt near the large metal sink, she stopped beside him, and like him regarded the broad trail of blood on the floor. Protruding from the sink was a length of corroding copper pipe, and with recognition 3 picked it up, noting the blood speckled on its end.

Both of them turned to follow the still wet smears with their eyes. Like one long, continuous brushstroke, the blood formed a pathway to the closed confession room door.

Still carrying the metal pipe, 2 bolted forward again, and 3 again followed, but this time she didn't voice a protest.

"It isn't just 5 and 6," the math teacher panted to himself as he ran, as if desperately working out a mysterious equation. "I know that…I *know* it. There were more of us…had to be. Missing numbers…there are missing numbers…"

Without hesitation, when he reached the door 2 flung it open wide and stepped inside the confessional.

Looking past his body, 3 cried out in shock.

A web of strands like extruded black slime filled the room, each strand originating from one of the graffiti-covered walls, with their other ends converging on a human body lying facedown on the floor, where it had been pulled out of the office chair. But they only saw this individual from the waist down. The upper potion of the body had been pulled through one of the painted walls…and as 2 and 3 gawked in horror, the body inched forward a little bit more. Then a little bit more, in another jerk of movement, as if someone on the other side of the wall were pulling the body through. The victim's legs were unmoving, and they couldn't tell if this person were still alive.

2 started forward, and 3 immediately latched onto him, fighting to hold him back despite his much greater size. "What are you doing?" she exclaimed.

"I've got to try to pull her out!"

"Don't touch her! She has that goop all over her…you can't let it touch you!"

"You saved me, remember? We've got to try to save her, too! It's 5 – you see? You *know* her!"

"It's too late…look!"

Another tugging jerk, and the motionless body was drawn through the solid material of the wall to the point of its knees. Another jerk, to the point of its calves. Then only the feet from the ankles down protruded from the wall. A final pull forward, and the sneakers passed through the wall as if it were only a holograph.

Now severed, all the cords that had been affixed to the body dropped limply like the lines of a landed parachute, only squirming weakly. Even as they fluttered downward, they began to evaporate.

"That was 5," 2 panted heavily, close to tears. "Say it!" He whirled at 3 with eyes blazing in a florid face. "Say it! That was 5! Say that you know her! *Say it!*"

She only stared back him mutely, as if she had suffered a traumatic head wound. Suffered amnesia. She switched her gaze past him, toward the empty office chair positioned under the room's single bare light bulb. Lying on the blood-stained linoleum floor beside the chair were a pair of eyeglasses with white frames.

In a flat voice, 3 said, "I ought to do my confession while I'm here."

"*What?*" 2 blurted. "Are you crazy?" He pointed toward the spot where the legs had been sucked into the wall. "Didn't you see what happened to her? We have to get out of this room! Out of this fucking building!"

"We have to complete the test."

"Complete the *test?*"

She looked at him again, eyes flat as her voice. "That's why we're here, isn't it? You agreed to the test. You signed a contract. This is important work being done."

"Honey…honey, you don't know what you're saying! Please…don't talk like this…"

"I'm going to do my confession now."

"There's no one listening in here! They were just having us come in here to…to soften us up, until we were psychologically ready, and maybe ready from the drugs, so we could be…assimilated! You saved me, remember? You were afraid for me when you saw them trying to take me!"

"I'm going to do my confession now," 3 repeatedly blandly. "Then you need to do your confession, too."

2 shook his head slowly, no longer able to hold back his tears. "No. I'm not doing any more confessions…and neither are you." And with that, he spun toward the closest of the four painted walls and swung the bloodied copper pipe.

The elbow at the end of the pipe rang off the glazed bricks. 2 felt the vibration sing up his arms. He struck the wall again, again, crying out as he did so, heedless of 3 behind him. She stepped away to avoid his backswing, but stretched her arms as if to catch hold of him. "Stop it!" she shouted. "Don't do that!"

Slowly he was chipping pieces from the wall, chunks that clattered at his feet, exposing the red meat of the bricks beneath. When he felt he had marred this wall enough for the time being, he moved on to the next. He had gone from yelling to grinning with sadistic delight, as if he were beating a living enemy. As if he were erasing figures from a mathematical equation of inhuman complexity. Each and every tiny 0 and 1 in these compositions had to be vital. Even these small wounds he was inflicting would disrupt the formulae. Just one gear removed from the machine and it would stop…it had to…

"Don't!" 3 shrieked. "You can't do this! God damn it, stop!"

He ignored her, moved on to the third wall. His bones were jarred, the muscles in his arms aching, but he battered gouges from the third wall and moved on to the fourth, which contained the doorway. He struck at the mural to one side of it, then the other. Every wall in the confessional was wounded now. "This room is where we go in," he ranted between blows. "It's where they absorb us. And then, those things…those black things come out, from one of the other murals." Another metallic, clanging blow. A tiny shard of brick ticked off his eyelid. "They're all that's left of us…like waste product…and then even that's gone!"

"You're talking insane, like someone's trying to kill us!"

"Not kill us – make us not exist!"

"You're wrong! Stop it…you're wrong!"

Heaving with heavier pants than even before, 2 halted his attack and turned to her. "What do you mean? What do you know?"

Her gaze was level and calm. "Change us, yes, I'm sure. Not destroy us…only make us better." She proffered a hand. "Let me have that thing."

Tears began flowing down 2's sweat-filmed face again, and he clutched the pipe close to his chest. "No."

She didn't lower her arm. "Okay…okay, then, if it makes you feel safer. But let's go rest now, okay? Let's go lie down. I'll lie down with you." That flat smile – was it meant to be seductive? "You're too stressed out; you're getting hysterical. Come lie down with me, and after you rest we'll talk about all this more rationally."

2 studied her, through tears so heavy that her form blurred. "Rest where?" he wheezed. "You think I'm going to lie down in those rooms with the artwork? No way. If you want to rest with me, we'll go back upstairs – where we slept last night."

"All right, honey, that's fine." Still the extended hand. "Let's go upstairs, then."

2 hesitated, his thoughts a kaleidoscope – a dizzying, scintillating kaleidoscope of only black and white – but then he stepped toward her and said, "Okay…okay."

11

A fluttering of living shadow behind 2's eyelids, and he woke with a start, fearing that the world was in flux – but it was only the fluorescent tubes in the ceiling. One had gone out totally, the other dying, its light fluctuating as if a glowing white liquid sloshed around inside. How long had he been asleep? So long that fluorescent light tubes, previously steady, might expire?

3 lay asleep beside him, covered to her chest in a sleeping bag. He had had trouble becoming aroused, but she had persisted, patient and determined, and eventually he had attained a climax that barely shook him, more of a meager release. Before this he might have caressed her hair or held her head as she pleasured him, but he had only looked on at her as if through someone else's eyes. He looked at her similarly now. In the unstable light, her skin appeared darker to him. On her exposed upper right arm, a single tattooed word he had somehow only noticed at this moment: ONE.

He hadn't expected to sleep again so soon after they'd awoken, but maybe she was right: his hysteria had exhausted him. He had thought to merely feign sleep until she herself dozed off, but had nodded off himself soon enough. He slipped out of his own sleeping bag as stealthily as possible so as not to wake her, dressed, then sat on one of the chairs to tie his sneakers. Standing, he retrieved his metal pipe. The blood was dry, and its end was now marked with paint from the murals.

He went to the emerald green door, which he had left open enough for him to steal through without having to move it, the rasping sound of which would surely wake her…and when he entered the hallway outside, he had all he could do to keep from shouting his surprise.

This broad hallway still bore its large composite windows on either side, its ceiling still flaking away and the floor covered in these fallen flakes, like a carpet of autumn leaves. The radiators against the walls here and there were still encrusted with rust. But every available inch of both walls was covered in black and white graffiti.

This had been done while they slept, vulnerable with the door partly open.

Reining in his trembling outrage, his horror, 2 glanced back through the doorway at the lumpen shape of his lover. He considered dragging the door closed, and quickly shoving the copper pipe through the door's handle so that 3 couldn't pull it open on her side. That way, she couldn't try to stop him again. He would come back for her, but first he would find a way out of here, or even find these hidden researchers, this Dr. Onsay, and force them to let him and 3 leave this place. But no…no…he couldn't lock her in. If something happened to him, then she would be trapped.

So he stalked down the newly painted hallway, leaving the green metal door open behind him.

****

3 lifted her head a little and cracked her eyes. It was she who had been feigning sleep. She considered going after 2 to stop him, but decided not to oppose him. Though it hurt

her that he didn't trust her, she still had faith that the two of them could find their path to togetherness.

She wriggled out of her sleeping bag like a snake shedding its skin. Without bothering to dress, she selected one of the vinyl-padded chairs corralled in the corner, and dragged it to the very center of the room below the sickening, extinguishing light.

****

When he had emerged from the other end of the hallway and entered the stairwell, 2 had found the walls here wholly filled with graffiti as well.

He had descended to the ground floor, and here too discovered that every wall had been painted in what appeared like wild collisions of black and white, but he already knew how unthinkably, intentionally elaborate it all was. An architecture within this architecture.

He had broken into a run, graffiti flashing past him as though he were plummeting through space, past constellations and nebulae in swirls and soundless explosions. Words and names he couldn't decipher for their distortions, if they were truly words and names at all. Infernal order disguised as mindless chaos.

He had burst into the banquet hall, with its walls formerly composed of glazed white brick.

Here, each wall was freshly masked with black and white graffiti all the way to the high ceiling.

That had been hours ago...he didn't know how many.

More of the fluorescent tubes throughout the complex had died out, and day was on the wane, wintry light glowing blue outside windows large and small. In frustration, he used his metal club to smash one window between its bars, and called outside, "Help! Help us! Help!"

His breath steamed in the icy air, which lashed at his face as if to force his words back into him.

He located doors that he felt must lead outside, but when he pulled on them he would find them unmovable, probably padlocked on the other side. Possible fire exits…two garage doors in what had to have been a loading dock…various others: all locked.

He came upon one door in what was apparently a reception area or front vestibule, and here the padlock was on the inside, heavy and brand new.

His explorations took him further and further, into areas he had never visited before. He climbed stairs when he chanced upon them, then descended back to ground level again later. He ventured anywhere there was sufficient light to see, but avoided corridors and chambers that were swallowed in complete darkness. As evening progressed, such areas became more abundant.

Everywhere he explored, it was the same. After hours of seeking a means of escape, seeking enemies he was convinced meant their guinea pigs harm, it was clear that every last wall in the complex – apart from the makeshift storage room where he had left 3 – had been swept by the tide of graffiti. It no longer seemed to him that people were painting these walls, but that the graffiti was generating itself, picking up momentum as it spread like a virus.

This isolated microcosm…this insulated pocket universe…was a drowned world, black water having poured through every crack or chink to fill it utterly. He knew it wanted to drown him, too.

So just as a shark will drown if it stops swimming, he kept on moving, ignoring exhaustion, ignoring thirst and hunger. Once he stopped to relieve his bladder – maliciously, on one of the endless murals that had made this formerly disparate group of connected structures into something much more homogenous.

He was zipping his fly when a peripheral movement across the mid-sized room in which he stood caused him to look in that direction. Close to the floor, two glossy black arms had reached out of a wall, scrabbling blindly at the cement floor. The smooth top of a hairless head emerged, followed soon by the head in its entirety. It lifted as if to regard 2 in turn, but it had no eyes, and only a stretched depression instead of a mouth giving vent to a throat. This creature was not able to scream, but it began shaking its head in a mad blur, from side to side, as it dragged it shoulders from the wall…its torso…

"5?" 2 bellowed, to compensate for his fear. His voice bounced back at him in heavy ripples, distorted by the room's hollowness. He was backing toward the doorway. "5, is that you?"

In a last lurch forward, the entity pulled its legs out of the wall, loosely tethered by drooling strands, and promptly went into a kind of violent seizure, reminding 2 of a large fish tossed onto a ship's deck.

Whether or not the tormented being meant him any harm, he turned and fled from the room…hoping it would attain its inevitable disintegration before it came looking for him.

****

He went as far as the brick building across from that which contained the base camp, evidently the oldest unit of the complex, but after scouring its lighted areas in vain he began to make his way back again, still hoping to find an unlocked door to the outside he'd missed, or a window that had been overlooked by his keepers when the rest had been outfitted with new bars.

In a building somewhere between these opposing structures, he was sure he heard an almost subliminal humming sound. The first time he had passed through here he had thought he'd detected something, and now sure enough here it was again.

He rechecked the rooms he had explored before, even the upper levels, but as he ascended the humming diminished. On the ground floor once more, he did his best to track the sound and stood at last at the mouth of a tight corridor in pitch blackness. He cursed that he had no flashlight, no matches. But that sound…the more he stood listening to it, the more certain he became that it originated from somewhere at the other end of that inky hallway. In the end, he decided to venture down its throat, careful to shuffle along the midline of the corridor. He didn't want to trip on some debris and come into contact with the walls, which even though he couldn't see them were no doubt brimming with the ubiquitous graffiti.

At one point he stopped to glance behind him, and the mouth of the tunnel was a small pale rectangle. How much further did this hallway go?

But the more he moved ahead, the louder that humming became. Now it sounded more like a rumbling, such as that of a distant train passing through the night.

When the end of the tunnel came, he stepped into a large room without fluorescent lights, but a subdued blue glow entered through a row of large windows close beside him. He heard the delicate tick of icy snowflakes spitting against the panes, like the gentle scratching of ghostly children. But still, that humming rumble. He crossed the room, following the sound through a doorway in the far wall. Here, he came upon a stairwell – a flight of steps ascending, and another that descended to a basement level. The sound came from the latter.

Leaning over the handrail, he saw a feeble illumination at the foot of the cement stairs. He started down, and with each step the unbroken rumbling grew more pronounced. It was unmistakably the thrumming of machinery. Was this finally some of the machinery that had once been used in this place, if it had been a factory? Or was it a boiler room to provide the heat…a generator to supply the electricity?

At the bottom of the stairs, sure enough he entered a basement with pipes both thick and thin running along the low ceiling, supported by brackets and bound with greasy cobwebs. Spaced here and there, a few bare bulbs glowed. Their light glistened in reflection on the graffiti-painted brick walls, and in scattered puddles where water had dripped from spots where the pipes were bandaged like weeping wounds.

Down yet another tunnel-like hallway he followed the mechanical chugging, now a deep rapid throb like a titanic heartbeat that he felt vibrate up through his soles and disperse throughout his nervous system. Louder…louder…until he arrived at the source.

It was a doorway in the brick, covered with a barred gate. The bars were freshly painted, and he knew the gate had been added at the same time as the bars over the windows. He gave it a useless tug, having already spotted the chain and heavy padlock that secured the metal door in place.

Beyond the bars, the room was in darkness and thus he couldn't determine its size, couldn't guess at the appearance and hence the function of the machinery, or how extensive it was. All he could see from here was a constellation of scattered glowing buttons in a variety of colors – green, red, amber, blue, but their light was not enough to illuminate their surroundings. Set further back in the room, he was sure he saw a few pale blue computer monitors.

Computers! Might he use one of them to send emails to summon help?

He tried to break the chain with his copper pipe, wedging it between the coils and pulling on it like a lever, but the links were too thick. He couldn't fit the straight end of the pipe into the U-shaped shackle of the padlock, either. At last, in frustration, he hammered at the padlock using the pipe as a club. He only produced loud clanks and, once, a few spitting sparks. Exhausted as much psychologically as he was physically, he stumbled back from the gate, sucking at air, his throat and mouth feeling coated with sand, licking his parched lips.

He realized he needed to rest, to get his head together. Refreshed, he might gain fresh perspective, devise another plan. He needed water – food if he dared – and most of all, he was anxious to check in on 3. Surely she must have awakened by now. Finding him absent, might she even be looking for him? Despite her changed demeanor, he longed for her companionship. And so, he turned away from the mysterious machines behind the barred door, to find his way back to the storage room. To find his way to 3.

****

Some hours earlier, sitting nude as a newborn infant on the former banquet hall chair in the center of the room where they had made their new camp, 3 had spoken aloud in a one-sided discourse.

"It doesn't matter anymore about Seth…if I can't be sure of his love, then he was never important. It's time to move on. And there's no taking back what that priest did to me, our good old Father Ryan. After all, he's dead now, so it's all in the past. And my Mom…yes, it's hard, but she knew how much I love her, and I'll always have my memories – like watching *One Life to Live* in the hospital with her.

"We can't walk around with open bleeding wounds, can we? If we're ever going to get it together, and realize our full potential, we have to get on with our lives. No…we have to make a *new* life for ourselves. A better life.

She smiled. "This is a fresh start. I'm a phoenix."

Then she closed her eyes and tilted her head back, still smiling, waiting for 2 to come join her.

****

When 2 climbed the stairs out of the basement, he found the ground level's floor had been covered in graffiti. So had the ceiling.

"No," he said in disbelief. "Oh my God, no."

At first he was reluctant to set foot upon it. Might the paint be *all* there was, with nothing solid behind it? Not coating the floor, but in place of the floor? Might he fall straight through and plunge endlessly through fathomless space? Endlessly through some unknown dimension? But what choice did he have, if he wanted to get back to 3?

And so he started forward warily at first, step by step, as if crossing the melting ice of a frozen lake. But it was solid beneath his feet, solid as ever, and so he quickened his pace until he was running, huffing, running…

His transfigured environment disoriented him with its sameness. It became harder to distinguish ceiling from wall from floor, as if indeed he were moving through the depths of space. But eventually, after a number of wrong turns, he reached the base camp building – or wing, if the complex were all one vast structure – and when he entered the banquet hall saw that even here, the graffiti had spread to the floor. It covered the flat areas of the ceiling but had not affected its exposed metal beams and joists.

The PVC pipe running down the wall from a hole in the ceiling had not been affected, nor the bucket positioned beneath it, and as they were both white they stood out more distinctly than usual against their backgrounds. He rushed to the bucket, thinking he might risk eating one of those cereal bars because they were sealed in factory packaging. He even entertained the mad idea of smearing the cereal bar's raspberry filling on a wall, for want of paint – using it to write his name. Not the number 2, but his *name.* In an expression of defiance. In a declaration of identity.

When he looked into the bucket, he saw only one envelope of pills, and one stapled lunch bag, but he never even touched them, for something else caught his attention. He reached in and picked it up, befuddled and marveling and suspicious and elated all at once.

It was a single key linked to an emerald green plastic tag, like a hotel key. A number was printed on the plastic tag in metallic gold: 11.

What was this key for? To open the gated door in the basement, and give access to the machinery and the computers? Or better yet…oh yes, better yet…that padlock on the door it what had seemed to have once served as a front reception area?

Had the test come to an end, then? Dr. Onsay's needs fulfilled?

Grinning, 2 pocketed the key and straightened, glancing around him as if he expected to see Dr. Onsay emerge from a doorway, clapping his hands and congratulating him on a job well done. There was no one, but 2's gaze settled on the closed confessional's door. So far, at least, the graffiti had not spread to the surfaces of doors. He felt a compulsion he could not explain, urging him to go look inside, so he walked toward the door. Maybe he felt he needed to see if the walls in there were still marred from his attack. Maybe he believed, but he couldn't say why, 3 had come down here to defy him and make a confession. *No, please, not that*, he thought as he hastened his stride.

Opening the door, he saw the room was empty. Graffiti extended now to the ceiling and floor – obscuring the former blood stains – but the wounds he had gouged in all four walls were still there. Good. His gaze lowered to the pair of eyeglasses with white frames lying on the floor beside the chair. He couldn't recall to whom they had belonged, but after a moment of hesitation he went to them, retrieved them, folded the glasses and slipped them in his breast pocket. Then he left the room and continued on toward the storage room upstairs. His smile returned. He couldn't wait to show 3 the key…then take her with him to go test it. He trusted his intuition utterly now, had no doubt whatsoever that this key was the instrument of their freedom.

****

"Hey," he gushed, slipping past the still half-open green metal door, "hey –"

He stopped in his tracks on the graffiti-covered floor.

Somehow the graffiti had spread across the floor without affecting the strewn doll heads. The collection of unrolled sleeping bags. The group of chairs in one corner – and the chair that stood alone, and vacant, in the center of the room. The graffiti had crawled up and consumed the walls, the ceiling. The graffiti had created a new confession room.

"No," 2 choked. "Oh no." His body sagged. His soul sagged within him. He stepped further into the room, turned in a slow shambling circle. Perhaps she had simply gone out into the complex in search of him…perhaps if he just stayed here and waited for her to return…

His thoughts froze like a startled deer before it bursts into flight, when he heard a distant unearthly scream. It ululated, echoed with a watery resonance, rang in his ears and in the hollow of his chest. But ultimately, after only a few moments, it faded away and was gone.

2 dropped the copper pipe, and it clanged by his feet. He pressed the palms of his hands hard into his eye sockets, and released a single barking sob. He had never learned her name. He hadn't even known her name.

He backed up blindly, hands still crushing his closed eyes. He would not forget her. He swore he would not allow that to happen.

He backed against the chair at the midpoint of the room, and fell into a sitting position upon it. And still he blocked his eyes.

He sat that way for an indeterminate amount of time. It might not even have been a linear "arrow of time."

Then, he raised his head and lowered his hands from his eyes. He blinked, but perhaps from the pressure against them his eyes were blurry, so he reached into his breast pocket, withdrew his eyeglasses with their narrow lenses and fashionable white frames by Roberto Cavalli, and slipped them on. Yes, oh yes…much better.

Dr. Once twisted around a little on the chair's vinyl seat, this way then that, surveying the room. "Yes," he spoke aloud to the walls, as if making a confession to no one but himself. His voice bore only the barest tease of an accent. "Quite good." Water damaged, the scabby mottled walls looked diseased, but were at least completely devoid of graffiti.

He was more than satisfied. Like a Mobius strip

looping in on itself, the experiment was ended and had just begun.

Dr. Once rose from his chair, and before leaving the room – leaving the building – double checked that he still had the key in his pocket. He withdrew it, and fingered the green plastic tag, the tag which bore in metallic gold the number that was his name.

01010100011010000110010100100000010001010110111001100100

About the Author

Jeffrey Thomas is an American author of weird fiction, the creator of the acclaimed milieu Punktown. Books in the Punktown universe include the short story collections PUNKTOWN, VOICES FROM PUNKTOWN, PUNKTOWN: SHADES OF GREY (with his brother, Scott Thomas), and GHOSTS OF PUNKTOWN. Novels in that setting include DEADSTOCK, BLUE WAR, MONSTROCITY, HEALTH AGENT, EVERYBODY SCREAM!, and RED CELLS. Thomas's other short story collections include WORSHIP THE NIGHT, THIRTEEN SPECIMENS, NOCTURNAL EMISSIONS, DOOMSDAYS, TERROR INCOGNITA, UNHOLY DIMENSIONS, AAAIIIEEE!!!, HONEY IS SWEETER THAN BLOOD, and ENCOUNTERS WITH ENOCH COFFIN (with W. H. Pugmire). His other novels include LETTERS FROM HADES, THE FALL OF HADES, BEAUTIFUL HELL, BONELAND, BEYOND THE DOOR, THOUGHT FORMS, SUBJECT 11, LOST IN DARKNESS, THE SEA OF FLESH AND ASH (with his brother, Scott Thomas), BLOOD SOCIETY, and A NIGHTMARE ON ELM STREET: THE DREAM DEALERS. Thomas lives in Massachusetts.

Printed in Great Britain
by Amazon

42565576R00069